G000067772

RUNNI
TO LOVE

Barbara Cartland

Barbara Cartland Ebooks Ltd

This edition © 2020

ISBNs

9781788673211 EPUB

9781788673228 PAPERBACK

Book design by M-Y Books
m-ybooks.co.uk

THE BARBARA CARTLAND ETERNAL COLLECTION

The Barbara Cartland Eternal Collection is the unique opportunity to collect all five hundred of the timeless beautiful romantic novels written by the world's most celebrated and enduring romantic author.

Named the Eternal Collection because Barbara's inspiring stories of pure love, just the same as love itself, the books will be published on the internet at the rate of four titles per month until all five hundred are available.

The Eternal Collection, classic pure romance available worldwide for all time .

THE LATE DAME BARBARA CARTLAND

Barbara Cartland, who sadly died in May 2000 at the grand age of ninety eight, remains one of the world's most famous romantic novelists. With worldwide sales of over one billion, her outstanding 723 books have been translated into thirty six different languages, to be enjoyed by readers of romance globally.

Writing her first book 'Jigsaw' at the age of 21, Barbara became an immediate bestseller. Building upon this initial success, she wrote continuously throughout her life, producing bestsellers for an astonishing 76 years. In addition to Barbara Cartland's legion of fans in the UK and across Europe, her books have always been immensely popular in the USA. In 1976 she achieved the unprecedented feat of having books at numbers 1 & 2 in the prestigious B. Dalton Bookseller bestsellers list.

Although she is often referred to as the 'Queen of Romance', Barbara Cartland also wrote several historical biographies, six autobiographies and numerous theatrical plays as well as books on life, love, health and cookery. Becoming one of

Britain's most popular media personalities and dressed in her trademark pink, Barbara spoke on radio and television about social and political issues, as well as making many public appearances.

In 1991 she became a Dame of the Order of the British Empire for her contribution to literature and her work for humanitarian and charitable causes.

Known for her glamour, style, and vitality Barbara Cartland became a legend in her own lifetime. Best remembered for her wonderful romantic novels and loved by millions of readers worldwide, her books remain treasured for their heroic heroes, plucky heroines and traditional values. But above all, it was Barbara Cartland's overriding belief in the positive power of love to help, heal and improve the quality of life for everyone that made her truly unique.

AUTHOR'S NOTE

The fêtes and parties given by the Prince Regent at Carlton House became a legend for their fantastic extravagance and elaborate preparations.

Ever since the Prince Regent had moved into Carlton House, he had been building and increasing its size. Houses were demolished on either side and Carlton House enlarged. The extensive gardens extended from Pall Mall to Marlborough House.

At the time of one of H.R.H.'s parties *The Morning Post* reported that five hundred men had been at work for a month to produce the 'most brilliant fireworks ever seen in the country'.

At the first party the Prince Regent gave when he was Prince of Wales and allowed to have his own house, two thousand invitations were sent out for a fête in June.

By eight o'clock on the appointed day, Pall Mall, St. James's Street and the Haymarket were blocked with carriages, although guests were not invited until nine o'clock.

The proceedings were so brilliantly done that despite the crowds there was 'no hustle or bustle in waiting and everything was done as in a private house'.

Even those who had been in the rooms inside Carlton House before had not seen all the furniture, pictures and ornaments in them. The Prince Regent was continually improving his collections,

When he became King George IV in 1820 and moved to Buckingham Palace, most of his collection went with him.

I was, however, broken-hearted to learn that it was not until 1927 that Carlton House was pulled down, so I could have seen it. Unfortunately I did not write any historical novels until 1948.

There was no doubt that, despite his extravagances, the Prince Regent was a remarkable man.

He not only had extraordinarily good taste, but as he walked amongst his guests he was affable, amusing, brilliantly witty and undoubtedly charming.

One can only agree with someone at the time who said of him that 'he was graciousness personified'.

CHAPRER ONE
1812

Ivana walked quietly down the corridor towards the study.

She had come in from a walk in Hyde Park with her old Nanny, who had been with her since she was a child.

Outside the house she had seen a phaeton drawn by two well-bred horses.

She thought, unhappily, that they belonged to Lord Hanford.

He was a man she disliked exceedingly and was, she well knew, a bad influence on her stepfather.

The last time Keith Waring had gone out to dinner with Lord Hanford they had gambled afterwards and Keith Waring had lost thirty pounds to his Lordship.

This had meant that something else had to be sold from the house.

It was always the treasures that Ivana prized, because they had belonged to her mother.

She was wondering how, if it was Lord Hanford, she could persuade her stepfather to refuse to accept his next invitation to dinner.

She reached the study, which was a small room where they usually sat when they were alone.

She could hear a harsh somewhat vulgar voice speaking loudly.

Her heart sank, but there was nothing she could do about it.

She was just turning away to tiptoe away and back to her bedroom in case Lord Hanford asked to see her, when she heard him say,

"I want Ivana and I intend to have her!"

There was a pause.

Then Keith Waring replied,

"I have been trying to find a rich husband for her."

"You know perfectly well that I cannot offer her marriage," Lord Hanford answered, "but I will settle enough money on her so that she will never want again, in fact I was just thinking of one thousand pounds a year."

Again there was a pause.

Ivana stiffened and felt that she could not be hearing aright.

Then, to her horror, she heard her stepfather somewhat hesitantly say,

"And what about – me?"

"I have not forgotten you," Lord Hanford replied. "I will give you five thousand pounds, which will pay off your immediate debts and a thousand pounds a year for as long as Ivana and I are together. You will not get a better offer from anyone else."

Ivana held her breath.

Surely, she thought, her stepfather would tell Lord Hanford that his idea was degrading and impossible.

Instead of which she heard Keith Waring saying,

"I suppose as I am 'below hatches' I shall have to accept your offer."

"You would be a *damned* fool if you did not," Lord Hanford replied. "You will not get a better one."

There was no answer from Keith Waring and Lord Hanford went on,

"The sooner all this is settled the better. And I expect you feel the same as the duns are at the door."

"That is true enough," Keith Waring said plaintively, "but I doubt if Ivana will agree."

"She can hardly refuse, considering that you are her Guardian," Lord Hanford said. "You know as well as I do that by the law of the land a Ward has to obey her Guardian, whether she likes it or not."

"Ivana is very self-willed," Keith Waring muttered.

"You can leave her to me," Lord Hanford responded.

"I am quite certain that she will kick up a fuss," Keith Waring replied. "Perhaps it would be wise to give her something to make her more pliable."

"If a horse is difficult, I don't drug it," Lord Hanford retorted. "I give him a taste of the whip."

With the greatest difficulty Ivana prevented herself from screaming.

Then Lord Hanford went on,

"I have never yet failed to master a horse or, for that matter, a woman. So stop worrying and just do as I tell you."

"I am not going to tell Ivana what you are planning," Keith Waring remarked.

"Nobody has asked you to," Lord Hanford retorted.

There was a pause as if he was thinking it all out in his mind.

"All you will tell Ivana," he carried on, "is that you are coming to stay at my house in Hertfordshire. I will collect her in a phaeton and you will say you are following in another. When you don't turn up, I will console her from worrying over you."

Keith Waring sighed.

"I suppose you know what you are doing. When do you want her to be ready?"

"On Friday," Lord Hanford replied. "I will call here at about two o'clock after you have finished luncheon."

Ivana did not wait to listen any more.

On tiptoe she crept away from the door of the study, hearing, as she did so, Lord Hanford saying,

"Now we have settled all that, let's have a drink on it."

She well knew that he was a hard drinker and wondered if there was anything left in the decanters for them to drink.

She was afraid that her stepfather might emerge from the study and then see her.

She started to move as quickly as she could. She crossed the narrow hall and then ran up the stairs.

Since her mother had died, Nanny had slept in the room next to hers and now she burst in through the door.

As she expected, Nanny had taken off her bonnet and the shawl she had worn when they had gone for a walk in the Park.

She was sitting as usual at the table by the window and sewing something.

Ivana closed the door behind her and then stood still for a moment with her back against it.

"Nanny! *Nanny!*"

It was a desperate cry of anguish, the like of which Nanny had not heard since Ivana was a little girl.

She put down her sewing and rose to her feet.

"What's happened? What's upset you, dearie?" she asked.

Ivana ran across the room and, kneeling beside Nanny's chair, hid her face against her.

"Nanny! Nanny!" she cried again. "What am – I to – do? What – am I to – do?"

Nanny held her close.

She had loved Ivana ever since she was born and the doctor, ignoring the midwife, had put the baby into her arms.

"Whatever's upset you now, dearie?" she asked Ivana again.

Hesitatingly, her words tumbling over themselves, Ivana repeated to Nanny what she had just heard through the study door.

"I hate – Lord Hanford – *I hate him*, Nanny!" she cried. "When he – stares at me with that – look in his eyes, it – makes me feel sick! He has – only to – touch my hand to make me want to – scream!"

"It's the most disgraceful thing I've ever heard!" Nanny exclaimed. "And your poor dear mother'd turn in her grave, that's what she'd do."

"I know – but Step-Papa is – my Guardian."

"He's a wicked man. He's no right to think of acceptin' anythin' just so horrible and so degradin'!" Nanny snapped.

"It's – the money – you well know it's – the money," Ivana said. "He spends everything we possess – and now there is little left – to sell."

Nanny knew that this only too true.

Just yesterday she had ruminated tartly,

"If much more goes from this house, I'll wake up to find my bed's been taken from under me!"

All the pretty *objet d'arts* that Ivana's mother had collected so diligently over the years had been sold off long ago and the pictures, the Dresden china and even the Persian rugs on the floor had gone as well.

Ivana knew that for weeks the Bank had been demanding that something must be done about the overdraft, which was continuing to grow week after week and month after month and the Bank was becoming more and more aggressive.

The tradesmen's bills came in regularly with endless urgent messages attached to them demanding payment at once.

Ivana raised her head.

"I know what you are – thinking Nanny," she said, "and I will – die rather – than become the m-mistress – of any man, let alone Lord Hanford."

She stumbled over the word 'mistress' and then burst into floods of tears.

Nanny held her close.

"We'll find some way out of this," she said soothingly, "but only God knows what it can possibly be."

"How can God – let this – happen to me?" Ivana asked. "How – *can* He?"

Nanny was silent for a moment and and then she suggested,

"You'll have to run away, that's what you'll have to do!"

Ivana raised her head again.

She was so surprised at Nanny's advice that she had stopped crying, but the tears were still wet on her cheeks.

Her eyes widened as she asked,

"R-run away? But – where to – Nanny?"

"That's what I'm tryin' to figure out," Nanny answered. "You knows as well as I do that there's no money for us to travel North to what relatives you have left and there's few enough of them at any rate."

Ivana knew only too well that what Nanny was saying was indeed true.

She had known when her mother had died that there were practically no relatives at the funeral.

Now that she was an orphan, she was very much alone.

Her beloved father, the Honourable Hugo Sherard, had been tragically killed at the Battle of Salamanca fighting against Napoleon in the Peninsula.

Her mother had been broken-hearted and for a year she had hardly spoken to anyone or taken any interest in anything that was going on around her.

Then Keith Waring had come into her life.

Although Ivana despised him, she had to admit to herself that he had made her mother, if not happy, comparatively content.

The Sherards came from Penrith in the North of England and her father's brother, who was a good deal older than Hugo, had succeeded to the title of Lord Sherard.

He had written her mother a letter when her father had been killed and he had written to Ivana when he had learned of her mother's death.

He had not, however, suggested that she should go to the North and live with him and his family.

She knew that he had a wife and children of his own and he doubtless had no wish to house an impoverished relative, besides which, it was a very long way to drive up to Penrith in the County of Cumberland.

At the moment anyway it would be impossible for her and Nanny to pay the fares they would be charged by one Post-chaise after another on the way North.

Ivana could think of none of her father's friends who would wish to take her into their homes.

After her mother had married Keith Waring, she had not kept in touch with those friends she had known when they had lived in the country. Instead she knew only those people who her husband had introduced to her in London.

It was with her money that they had rented the house in Islington.

It was the furniture that had belonged to Hugo Sherard which was arranged in the small and, Ivana thought, rather pokey rooms.

Because they were in London, it enabled Ivana to attend a Seminary for young ladies to complete her education

She and her mother had also visited Museums and Art Galleries, which she had enjoyed a great deal.

Now that she thought of it, the only people they entertained had been the rather raffish friends of her stepfather.

And the majority of them were men.

"Where can we – go, Nanny?" she asked again this time in a whisper.

"I'm just thinkin'," Nanny answered.

"Perhaps – as we have – no money at all," Ivana proposed, "I ought to – try and find some – work to do."

"I'm not havin' you doin' menial tasks," Nanny countered, "not while I'm alive!"

"But we have to eat – and food costs money," Ivana pointed out in a practical tone.

She sat back on her heels and then crossed her arms over Nanny's knees.

"Now let's think this out carefully," she said. "We have to think quickly, because it is now Tuesday and that leaves only – two days before that – ghastly man will take me away in his – phaeton."

The terror in her voice was very obvious and Nanny was aware that she was trembling.

She was not surprised.

Lord Hanford, she knew, was well over forty and he had already had two wives.

Although she had no intention of telling Ivana, it was rumoured that he was responsible for his second wife being certified as a lunatic.

The servants had gossiped that it was because he treated her in the same cruel way as he did his horses.

"There must be – something that I – can do," Ivana was saying. "After all I have had an extensive education and – "

She stopped and gave a little cry.

"But, of course!" she exclaimed. "I did the accounts in the country when Papa was in the War and, after he was killed, Mama left everything to me. I could be a secretary!"

Looking at her, Nanny thought it was very unlikely that anyone who looked as lovely as Ivana would be employed by a woman.

And if a man should do so, it would undoubtedly be dangerous.

"Perhaps," she said after a moment, "you could be a reader to an elderly lady. After all they needs someone to read to them when they're gettin' old and goin' blind and you have a really lovely reading voice."

"That is what Mama used to say," Ivana answered. "I would read the Collects to her on a

Sunday and then the poems of Lord Byron. They made her cry because they reminded her of Papa."

She sighed deeply and recalled how happy she had been reading to her mother before Keith Waring came into her life.

Then, as if forcing herself to be practical, she asked Nanny,

"How can I find out if there is a position out there waiting for me? Would there be an advertisement for a reader in the newspapers perhaps?"

"You have to go to an Employment Agency, dearie," Nanny replied. "I'll try and find out from Mrs. Bell downstairs which is the best one in London."

When they first came to London, Mrs. Bell had been engaged to clean the house and help Nanny with the cooking.

Nanny was a very good cook and had started to cook when they had been in the country.

After she was bereaved, Mrs. Sherard had to be tempted to eat anything and, after they came to London, Nanny had continued cooking because she enjoyed it so much.

What was more she was far cheaper than anyone else they could have employed.

Mrs. Bell charged very little for coming to the house for only two or three hours every morning. She cleaned out the fireplaces, scrubbed the floors and made the beds.

"Yes, ask Mrs. Bell," Ivana said, "and ask her quickly, Nanny, because there is no time to lose."

She felt a sense of terror surging through her body and it was making her feel incredibly agitaed.

Every minute was drawing her closer and closer to the moment when Lord Hanford, with his red face and his swimming eyes, would pull her roughly into his phaeton beside him and drive her away to unmitigated hell.

He would carry her away to the country where she would be imprisoned and never have any chance of escape.

Nanny rose from her chair.

"Now, you sit here," she said, speaking as if Ivana was three years old, "and be careful, if your stepfather comes in here not to let him know what you have overheard him talkin' to Lord Hanford."

"No, of course – not," Ivana said, "but hurry – do hurry – Nanny, I am frightened – I am terribly – frightened!"

Nanny went from the room and Ivana sat down in the chair that she had vacated and put her hands over her eyes.

How can this have happened?

How could the future be so degrading and so utterly abominable and menacing?

It was like being a dark room that she would never be able to escape from.

She knew well that her stepfather was a weak character and he was quite incapable of making money, only of losing it at the gaming tables.

He had, however, she had to admit even now at this time of terror, been really in love with her mother.

That was not so surprising since Mrs. Sherard had been exceedingly beautiful and lovely in every sense of the words.

There had been a great many men in love with her before she had met the Honourable Hugo Sherard.

They had both fallen in love with each other virtually at first sight and been ecstatically happy.

Years later, the Dragoon Guards, the Regiment that he was serving in, was sent to the Peninsula to fight for his King and country. They had formulated a brilliantly conceived plan to attack Napoleon where he might least have expected it.

However, after less than a year abroad, Hugo Sherard was killed.

At first Ivana thought that her mother would die too from grief and anguish.

Then, when she had seemed to be fading away and becoming weaker and weaker, Keith Waring appeared.

He was indeed an exceedingly handsome young man and because of his looks he had been spoilt dreadfully by every woman who had ever met him.

And Mrs. Sherard was no exception.

He was so very different from her first husband that in a way she mothered him.

She could not resist him when he finally declared that he would die if she did not marry him.

Ivana realised that it was a sacrifice on his part because he could, if he had wished, marry someone far richer and more prestigious.

But he genuinely loved her mother.

That, however, did not prevent him from spending every penny she possessed without thinking at all what the consequences would be.

Ivana had never liked him. She knew that he thought of her as just an encumbrance and resented the affection that her mother very obviously had for her.

From one or two things he had said recently she knew that he was thinking that, if he could find her a rich husband, he would be able to get her off his hands.

He would also undoubtedly line his own pockets to gamble with at the same time.

She never in her wildest imagination, however, thought that he could stoop so low as to 'sell her' to someone as unpleasant and dislikeable as Lord Hanford.

Lord Hanford was immensely rich that was undeniable and he could easily buy whatever he desired just by lifting his little finger.

Equally she could imagine how completely horrified both her father and mother would be at such despicable behaviour.

How could she contemplate the idea of living with a man without being married to him?

'How can I possibly – do anything so – humiliating?' she thought bitterly to herself.

She heard a footstep outside the door and was apprehensive for a moment that it was her stepfather.

But it was Nanny who came bustling into the room.

Because Ivana had jumped instinctively to her feet and was looking terrified, Nanny said soothingly,

"It's all right, dearie, he's gone out with his Lordship. He left a message with Mrs. Bell that he will not be back for luncheon or dinner."

Because they had been counting every farthing that was spent in the household lately, Ivana could not help thinking that this would save two meals.

Nanny closed the door behind her.

"I've found out what we wants to know," she said. "The best Agency be Mrs. Hill's on Mount Street."

"That is some distance away," Ivana remarked.

"I know," Nanny said, "but if you've got to work for anyone, I'll see to it as you works for the best!"

"Shall we go there at once?" Ivana asked.

"You'd better have your luncheon first," Nanny said. "There be no hurry, the Master won't be comin' back till the early hours of the mornin', if I knows anythin' about him."

"Oh, Nanny, I do hope he does not lose any more money," Ivana remarked.

As she spoke, she thought that if she was going to run away, it would no longer matter to her what happened.

Because Nanny expected it, Ivana went downstairs to the small dining room.

She had once suggested that, as Nanny did the cooking, she could sit in the kitchen.

Nanny would not hear of it.

"So long as I'm here you'll eat in the dinin' room, like the lady you are and behave like a lady and no nonsense about it!" she had asserted tartly.

Ivana helped herself to the cold chicken salad that Nanny had prepared for her earlier in the day.

She could not help wondering, when she was no longer a 'lady', if she would eat in the servants' hall.

She did not say so to Nanny, however, because she knew how much it would upset her.

She finished most of the salad even though she was far too agitated to be feeling in any way hungry.

Then she ran upstairs to put on the pretty bonnet she had worn when they went walking in the morning.

Nanny was a great believer in fresh air. She had always insisted on Ivana walking in the Park at some time during the day.

As Ivana came downstairs, she found that Nanny had also put on her bonnet and her grey shawl was draped over her shoulders.

"Now, put your best foot forward," Nanny urged her. "The walk'll do you no harm on such a nice day."

"No, of course not," Ivana agreed, "but I wish we could do it in the country."

She paused before she added,

"I suppose, Nanny, we could not just – disappear into the country and find a tiny cottage – where we could be on our own?"

"And how would we pay the rent?" Nanny enquired.

There was no answer to that and she went on,

"The only country we knows, you and me, is Huntingdonshire, where we were so happy when you were a child. And you may be quite sure if you're missin', that'll be the first place your stepfather'll look."

"Yes, of course, I did not think of that," Ivana admitted in a small voice.

They walked briskly because, although Nanny had turned fifty, she was still very fit.

It took them nearly three-quarters of an hour to reach Mount Street in Mayfair.

It was not difficult to find Mrs. Hill's Domestic Agency, which was on the first floor of No. 19.

There was a shop window in the front and beside it there was a door, which was open, revealing a narrow stairway.

Nanny stopped and Ivana asked her a little nervously,

"Are you coming in with me, Nanny?"

Nanny shook her head.

"That'd be a mistake," she replied. "Them as is lookin' for employment don't take their Nannies with them! Now you go up, dearie, and try not to be nervous. I'll be in the street lookin' in the shop windows."

Feeling as though she were very small and unprotected, Ivana climbed up the staircase.

There was a small landing and on one door there was a sign, which read,

MRS. HILL'S DOMESTIC AGENCY.

She opened the door and saw that there were several wooden benches inside against the wall.

On them were seated two rosy-cheeked young girls obviously up from the country. She guessed that they must be in search of suitable work like herself.

There was also an elderly man who might have been a coachman who was getting too old for his job.

At the far end of the room there was a high desk that had been painted in a dull beige colour.

Seated at it was an elderly woman wearing a red wig and blue spectacles. She looked so strange that Ivana stared at her, thinking that this surely could not be Mrs. Hill?

If she was staring, so was Mrs. Hill.

After a moment she said in a somewhat high-pitched voice,

"This way, madam, if you please."

Ivana realised that she was speaking to her.

Then, as she walked towards the desk, she understood.

Mrs. Hill had mistaken her for a would-be employer, who was visiting the Agency and not an employee.

This idea was confirmed when, as she reached the tall desk, Mrs. Hill, looking down at her, asked,

"And what can I do for you, madam? I suspect it's a lady's maid you'll be wanting?"

With an effort Ivana made herself speak,

"No," she replied, "I am not wishing to engage anyone but to be engaged."

Mrs. Hill drew a deep breath and there was a different expression in the eyes behind the blue spectacles.

Her voice had now sharpened as she asked,

"What sort of position do you require, might I ask?"

"I was wondering if you had a vacancy for a reader or perhaps a secretary."

Mrs. Hill gave a disdainful sniff before she opened a large ledger that was lying on the desk in front of her.

"I would very much doubt if we have any position like that available for *you*," she then said in a pointed tone.

"Oh, please, try and find one," Ivana insisted. "I am very eager to find employment and I have been told that you are not only the best Agency in the whole of London but you are also brilliant at finding applicants what they require."

As she spoke, she felt that she was almost being prompted by someone mysterious on what she should say.

There was no doubt that the flattery was succeeding.

Mrs. Hill turned over two or three pages and then said in a more conciliatory manner,

"Well, I'll have a good look, but I'm not that optimistic."

It was then a woman appeared from behind the desk.

She was in every way very different from Mrs. Hill. She was small and looked somewhat crushed. Her hair was grey, turning white, and she obviously made no effort to disguise her age.

In a low rather humble manner she suggested,

"I think, perhaps, you should look at page number nine, Mrs. Hill."

Mrs. Hill flipped over the pages impatiently.

"Don't be so ridiculous, Hetty," she said. "You know as well as I do they're looking for a man."

"We haven't been able to find one," Hetty replied, "and I just thought this young lady might be able to speak French."

"I think that's unlikely," Mrs. Hill snapped.

"On the contrary," Ivana interposed. "I speak French fluently. In fact as well as I speak English."

Mrs. Hill stared at her.

"If you're telling me a lie," she threatened ominously, "I'll not forgive you in a hurry."

"I am telling you the truth," Ivana said. "I was brought up with some French children and therefore I really am very fluent in French."

"I suppose you've forgotten," Mrs. Hill said as if she must have the very last word, "that they're our enemies! We should have nothing to do with the French or that monster Napoleon Bonaparte!"

Ivana was wondering what to reply.

Mrs. Hill, however, after almost glaring at her, looked down again at the ledger.

"It's been on the books for almost two weeks now," the woman called Hetty whispered, "and we still haven't found anyone to send them."

"Very well," Mrs. Hill said. "Be it on your own head and don't blame me if this young woman's turned away with a rude message."

"If it is a question of speaking French," Ivana intervened, because she thought that Hetty was being crushed, "I promise you that the lady or gentleman who requires a reader to speak French will be perfectly satisfied."

Mrs. Hill sniffed again.

"Pride goes before a fall!" she quoted loftily.

She wrote something down on a card that she had in front of her, paused and then handed it to Ivana.

"That's the address," she said, "and this is who you should ask for on arrival. If you're not accepted, it won't be worth your while coming back here."

"I understand," Ivana said. "Thank you very much for being so kind. I am very grateful."

She smiled at the woman called Hetty and said to her,

"And thank you so much too. "

Holding the card in her hand, she walked across the room to the door.

Two more older-looking servants had come in while she had been talking and taken their seats just inside the door.

One was a man and, as she approached, he rose and opened the door for her.

"Thank you," she said, thinking he looked like a butler.

"Good luck!" he muttered and she smiled back at him.

Going down the stairs, she stepped out onto the pavement and looked round for Nanny.

For one frantic moment she thought that she had disappeared. Then she saw her a little farther down the road, admiring some expensive china in a shop window.

She ran up to her.

"Nanny! *Nanny!*" she cried. "I've been told there is someone who needs a secretary who can speak French."

"Well, that's somethin' you can do, dearie," Nanny smiled. "So where is it?"

Ivana then looked down at the card in her hand for the first time.

Then she stared at it with an expression of surprise on her face that made Nanny ask,

"What is it? What's wrong?"

"I-I suppose it is – all right," Ivana said hesitatingly, "but – where we have to go is to the War Office – and ask for the Earl of Lorimer."

"Are you sure?" Nanny queried.

She inspected the card for herself and then commented,

"Well, as it's the War Office, I suspect they wants secretaries who can speak French to translate messages and speak to the French prisoners."

"Oh, of course!" Ivana then exclaimed. "And they'll want people to translate the secret documents they capture on the battlefields and things like that."

"I don't suppose that'll be too difficult a task for you," Nanny said, "but I don't like to think of you workin' alongside a lot of men."

"Why not?" Ivana enquired of her. "You can hardly expect the War Office to employ only women!"

She was suddenly still.

"I have just thought," she said in a different tone. "Mrs. Hill said that they had asked for a man. But, as they have been unsuccessful in finding one so far, they – might well give me – a chance."

It was obvious now that Mrs. Hill had been almost positive that she would be refused the position.

As if Nanny knew what she was thinking, she observed,

"There's no harm in tryin' and, if they sends you away, we'll just have to try another Agency. You can't expect to land on your feet the first time you takes a jump!"

It was so like Nanny to say something like that that Ivana laughed.

"How do we get to the War Office?" she asked.

"We takes a Hackney carriage, that's how," Nanny said, "and no nonsense about it. If we hangs about too long, if I knows anythin' about those office people, they'll all be goin' home and the place'll be locked up."

Ivana knew that this was sensible of Nanny. At the same time she could not help feeling that it was rather extravagant to hire a Hackney carriage to take them to the War Office.

Nanny, however, insisted and they found a Hackney carriage waiting at the end of the street.

When they told the driver where to go, he seemed impressed. He whipped up his tired old horse and they set off at a quick pace into Berkeley Square.

Nanny was looking out of the window to see where they were going.

Ivana, however, was holding the card that Mrs. Hill had given her tightly in her hand and praying.

'Please, God,' she prayed, 'please let them employ me. I would do anything – anything rather than have to do what my stepfather – wants of me and go – away with that – wicked and cruel old man.'

Even to think of Lord Hanford now made her tremble again.

Nanny put her hand over hers.

"It's goin' to be all right, dearie," she said, "I feels it in my bones and if the worse comes to the worst, we'll run away together and scrub doorsteps. It's somethin' I've done before when I was somewhat younger and I suspects that I can do it again."

Ivana laughed as Nanny had meant her to do.

"I am sure your doorsteps will be much cleaner than mine, Nanny," she replied.

CHAPTER TWO

The Hackney carriage finally stopped outside a large impressive-looking building.

For the first time Ivana looked nervous and was feeling nervous.

"Come with me, Nanny," she begged her.

Nanny shook her head.

"No, dearie," she said. "That would be a mistake. Secretaries don't have chaperones with them. I'll wait out here. We'll be ever so extravagant and keep the cab."

Slowly Ivana descended the steps of the carriage and then walked in through the door of the War Office.

A soldier in very smart uniform with highly polished brass buttons was standing beside a desk.

Ivana realised that he was waiting for her to explain why she was there. She held out the card that Mrs. Hill had given her.

He looked at it and, because he was reading it slowly, it seemed as if minutes passed before he said,

"I'll have you taken to his Lordship."

He snapped his fingers and another soldier, who looked very young, almost a pageboy, rose from where he was sitting in the background.

"Take this applicant to the Earl of Lorimer," the first soldier said sharply.

The boy took the card from him and started to walk ahead, obviously expecting Ivana to follow him.

They walked for what seemed to her for miles along corridors, up staircases and along more corridors.

Then they went down some stairs again before they came to what she thought must be the more important rooms on the ground floor.

She was sure of it when she saw two soldiers obviously on duty in the next corridor that they approached.

They walked past them and then, almost at the end of this particular corridor, the soldier who was guiding her stopped.

He knocked on a door and a deep voice called out,

"Come in."

The soldier went in by himself and Ivana realised that she was not to follow him.

He half-closed the door, leaving it open just enough so that she could hear what went on inside.

She heard him click his heels and she thought that he must have saluted.

The same deep voice that had said 'come in' then asked the soldier,

"What is it?"

"An applicant from the Agency, my Lord," the soldier replied.

He must have handed over the card because there was silence for a moment.

Then the deep voice ordered,

"Send him in."

Ivana realised at once that he was expecting a man and her heart sank.

As Mrs. Hill had said, the request had been for a man and she was sure that as a woman she would be rejected before any interview could even start.

The soldier came back to the door and opened it and then Ivana's chin went up and she walked into the room.

The soldier went out, closing the door behind him and she stood just inside the doorway, not certain whether she should wait or go forward.

The room was small and well-furnished with several comfortable chairs clustered round an empty fireplace

The Earl was sitting at a very large desk, piled high with copious papers.

When Ivana looked at him, she was surprised.

She had somehow expected him to be an old man with perhaps grey or white hair.

She had the idea that anyone in the War Office would be old because the young men would all have gone to fight the War.

But the Earl of Lorimer looked about thirty and was extremely handsome with dark hair brushed back from a square forehead.

As he went on writing, she could look at him without embarrassment. She thought at once that he had a hard face.

There was a squareness about his jaw and a firmness to his lips that told her he would be intent on getting his own way and his orders must be obeyed instantly. He would certainly fight to the end for anything he desired.

It seemed to her to be a long time before the Earl looked up and turned towards Ivana.

"Come and sit down," he said, indicating a chair on the other side of his desk.

He spoke sharply as if he was giving an order.

Then, when he saw to whom he was speaking, there was an astonished look in his eyes.

"I understand," he said after a moment, "that you have come here from the Agency."

"That is right," Ivana agreed. "Mrs. Hill sent me – to you."

She had reached the desk by this time and, as she was feeling shy, she sat down quickly on the chair as if she needed its support.

The Earl was still staring at her.

"Is this some sort of joke?" he asked and now his voice was hard, as if he thought that she was an intrusion on his space.

"No, no, of course not," Ivana replied quickly. "I came in response to your request for someone – who could speak French."

She then saw what she thought was an unbelieving look in the Earl's eyes.

Then, with hardly a pause, he started to speak to her very rapidly in French.

He asked her where she came from and how, when she was obviously English, she had learned to speak such good French.

Then he said he thought that she must be under a misapprehension regarding the whole matter. He spoke very fluently, but with just a trace of an English accent.

As soon as he had finished speaking, Ivana replied in what she knew was perfect Parisian French.

She told him, as she had told Mrs. Hill, that she had been brought up with some French children and she said that she had spoken French almost as soon as she could speak English.

She could read French and write in French and, if necessary, think in French.

"That was the sole reason," she explained, "why, since Mrs. Hill could not find a man for the position, she had come to see him."

As she finished speaking, she sat there with a defiant look on her face, knowing that it was impossible for him to find fault with her French.

The Earl unexpectedly laughed.

"You have proved your point," he said, "but now let us begin. Perhaps you will introduce yourself as there is no name on this card."

He dropped it on the desk as he spoke and Ivana thought that Mrs. Hill had deliberately not put her name on it in case, as a woman, she was turned away at the door.

"My name, my Lord," she replied, "is Ivana – "
She stopped.

It suddenly shot through her mind that it would be a mistake for her to give him her real name.

If she was to disappear completely, her name could be a certain clue that would put her once again into her stepfather's hands.

In the passing of a second she said the only name that came into her mind – and that was Nanny's.

" – Tate," she finished.

"Well, Miss Tate," the Earl replied, "you have very certainly proved that you can speak French, but I doubt if you could comply with the other attributes I require in the person I wish to engage."

Ivana drew a deep breath.

"What you are saying, my Lord, is that I should be a man, but Mrs. Hill made it clear that she has no man on her books who can speak French, nor did she think it likely that she would be able to find one."

The Earl frowned.

"It cannot be an impossible thing to ask," he exclaimed.

"I think, if you will forgive me saying so," Ivana replied, "that, even if people can speak French, they are not particularly keen at this very moment to advertise the fact. After all we are at war with France."

"I am aware of that," the Earl said coldly. "At the same time perhaps it does not trouble you."

"I had not thought of speaking French being an asset," Ivana answered, "until just a short while ago when I was in Mrs. Hill's Agency."

"And what position were you looking for from Mrs. Hill?" the Earl enquired.

"I thought," Ivana related frankly, "that I might be a reader to an old lady or perhaps a secretary. I have done quite a lot of secretarial work in the past in one way or another."

"I should have said," the Earl remarked, "looking at you, that either of those positions were most suitable."

There was silence between them and then Ivana began to feel that she had failed.

Then she pointed out,

"If you are thinking that I am too young to do what you require, it is something that will be rectified in time."

The Earl laughed.

"That is certainly true. Yes, Miss Tate, I was thinking that you are too young and so it would be difficult for anyone looking as you do to carry out my requirements."

"But you need somebody who can speak perfect French," Ivana argued.

"That is most unfortunately true," the Earl said, "and, as you already know, I am finding it hard to find anyone."

"Then, please – *please*," Ivana insisted, "give me a chance. I promise you that I am quite intelligent. I have been well educated and I am at present desperately in need of employment immediately."

The way she spoke was very revealing.

The Earl looked at her speculatively before he asked,

"Why should you be in such a hurry?"

"Because I have no money and nowhere to go," Ivana replied.

"Can that really be true?" the Earl enquired.

"I am an orphan," Ivana explained, "My mother died recently and my father was killed fighting Napoleon in the Peninsula."

"So your father was in the Army?"

"Yes."

"In what Regiment?"

Again it flashed through Ivana's mind that it might be dangerous to tell him the truth.

Then she told herself that the Army was a very large one.

It was highly unlikely that the Earl, even if he was in the War Office, would know the name of every acting Officer in every Regiment.

After a little hesitation, she answered him,

"The Fourteenth Dragoons."

"That is my own Regiment," the Earl informed her with a smile, "so perhaps I knew your father."

Too late Ivana realised that she had made a serious mistake.

"What was his name?" the Earl asked Ivana as she did not speak.

There was silence until she said,

"Please – we are not concerned with my – father – but with me."

"If you are to work for me," the Earl replied, "then I am concerned with every aspect of your life and past."

Ivana clasped her fingers together.

"I-I would rather remain – anonymous."

"I am afraid that is impossible," the Earl told her. "The position that concerns you is in fact a very important one. I would not be allowed, even if I wanted to, to employ anyone who I knew nothing about."

There was another long silence until Ivana, knowing that he was waiting for her to say something, replied,

"If I tell you – the truth – will it remain strictly secret?"

"It will remain a secret from everybody except myself and the Secretary of State for War who, as you will know, is Viscount Palmerston."

"You promise," Ivana insisted, "promise by everything you hold sacred?"

She saw an expression of surprise in the Earl's eyes.

Then his eyes twinkled before he responded,

"I give you my word as an Officer and, I hope, as a gentleman. I cannot believe that you will refuse it."

"No, of course not, my Lord, but it is very very important to me that no one should ever know where I am and what I am doing."

"So you have run away!" the Earl exclaimed.

"Yes, I have run away – from something horrible, disgusting, degrading and very very wicked!" Ivana retorted.

She spoke so violently that the Earl realised how much it meant to her.

Quietly he persisted,

"I have given you my word and, when you tell me your father's name, I promise that, with the exception of the Secretary at War, no one will know of it."

"My – my father was a Major, the Honourable Hugo – Sherard," Ivana said almost in a whisper.

"Then, of course, I knew him! Only not well, but I remember him being killed. We lost two other very fine Officers in the same engagement at Salamanca."

"My father was not afraid to die," Ivana said, "but it nearly destroyed my mother."

"And you say your mother is now dead?"

"She died two years ago," Ivana answered, "but not before she had married again."

The way she spoke made the Earl look at her penetratingly.

Then, as she did not say anything more, he quizzed her,

"I believe I am not mistaken in thinking that it is your stepfather who you are running away from?"

"I-I have to – I have to run away – so please – please let me work for you – but no one – *no one* must ever know where I am."

"I have already given you my promise," the Earl said, "but I suppose you would not like to tell me why you are running away from your stepfather?"

Ivana shook her head.

"I don't want to – speak of it to anyone – but I have to hide and – if you will not employ me – I must go back to Mrs. Hill – but she told me she had – nothing at all suitable for me on her books."

There was silence.

Then, because she was desperate, Ivana carried on,

"Please – please help me – if you knew Papa, you would know that he would tell me I was doing the – right thing in asking you for your help, my Lord."

The Earl smiled.

"You are making it difficult, Miss Sherard, for me to refuse you."

Ivana looked up at him with hope in her eyes.

"Do you mean you – really will employ me? Oh, thank you – *thank you*! I know that Papa would thank you too if he was still alive."

"I am not certain he would do that," the Earl said slowly, "because what I am going to ask you to do is both difficult and dangerous."

"Nothing could be more dangerous than the position I am in at the moment," Ivana said. "Nothing – not even if it was going into battle against the French cannon."

She spoke so vehemently and looked so lovely as she did so that the Earl guessed that there was a man concerned.

Aloud he said,

"Now let me explain to you, Miss Sherard, exactly what I want you to do. You must be absolutely frank with me and tell me if you think it is impossible or too frightening. I will understand and will promise to do my best to find you some other form of employment that would be suitable for you."

"I-I am listening," Ivana tried to smile.

The Earl rose from the chair that he was sitting in.

"As I wish to speak very confidentially," he began, "I suggest we sit on the sofa where we can be comfortable, although it is well-nigh impossible in the War Office where no one can overhear what we are saying."

He moved round the desk as he spoke and Ivana saw that he walked with a limp.

"You have been wounded!" she exclaimed.

"I should not be here otherwise," he said sharply. "I was wounded four months ago and I can assure you that as soon as I have recovered I shall return to my Regiment."

Now she could understand why anyone so young was working at the War Office.

She guessed that he had been given an important job because he was such an outstanding Officer and was obviously extremely intelligent.

The Earl, having reached the sofa, waited for Ivana to seat herself before he sat down as well.

She saw that one leg, which was in plaster, was stretched out in front of him.

He walked without a stick, but she was aware that he had touched two chairs as if for support on his way to the sofa.

Now she looked up at him and saw an expression in his eyes that she did not understand.

Then he said in a very quiet voice, almost as if he was speaking to himself,

"You are very young and very beautiful! Perhaps it is wrong of me to involve you in this."

"You have not yet told me what it is," Ivana retorted.

"I am thinking of you," the Earl replied. "But I know that my country must come first. I am therefore going to offer you this position, but don't forget you have the absolute right to reject it."

"I-I know."

"Then let me start from the beginning, I am sure you realise, as we do here at the War Office, that the end of the War is now in sight."

"I hope so – I sincerely hope so," Ivana said, "but – it will not bring back Papa."

"No, it will not do that," the Earl agreed, "but he will have died, as so many others have, for a great cause. Because England matters not only to us but to the world as well."

The way he spoke was very moving. Ivana just looked at him, her eyes raised to his and her long fingers clasped together in her lap.

With what seemed an effort the Earl went on,

"We believe that Bonaparte is growing desperate and, because he is desperate, he will do the unexpected. We therefore have to remain alert, otherwise it could be disastrous for us."

"I understand," Ivana said.

"That is why we at the War Office are perturbed at the arrival in England of the Marquis de Souvenant."

He paused for a moment, took a deep breath and then went on,

"Smugglers' boats are continually crossing over the English Channel however hard our Coastguards try to stop them from doing so."

"And the Marquis came here in one of them?" Ivana asked.

"He paid them, of course, saying that he was a refugee who had escaped from prison and desired only to help England to beat the Corsican, Napoleon, whom he loathes and despises and who is destroying his country."

"And you think that he does not really feel like that?" Ivana enquired.

"There is a certain doubt in my mind," the Earl replied, "although the majority of people concerned believe him to be entirely genuine."

"Nevertheless you are suspicious, my Lord."

"Shall I say I am being cautious," the Earl replied. "I have seen so many tricks played by Frenchmen during this War and I find it difficult to understand why the Marquis has taken so long to escape. Then why, having done so, does he wish to join us, the English, rather than the rebels against Bonaparte who undoubtedly exist in France?"

"I can see your reasoning," Ivana murmured.

"In any case," the Earl went on, "the Marquis is here. However I have to admit that he has given us some useful information that has proved to be correct."

"But you still feel that he is not to be trusted?"

The Earl put out his hands.

"I don't know," he said, "I have not met the Marquis, but what I have been told to do is to find him accommodation because he has no money. Also it is my Department who will look after him while he is here and accept any contribution he can make towards the advance of our troops."

"I understand," Ivana nodded, "and you want me to translate everything that he says in French into English."

The Earl shook his head.

"No. I want you to do something far more difficult than that."

Ivana looked at him enquiringly.

"I want you," the Earl said slowly, "to pretend that you speak not a word of French. You will then act as his secretary and write down anything he wishes you to do, but it must be in English."

"I-I don't understand," Ivana remarked.

"It is quite simple," the Earl answered. "If he gets in touch with any of the French here, and I can assure you there is a large contingent of them in England, then they will speak in their own language and you will understand every word of what is being said."

There was a silence before Ivana pointed out,

"Then – what you are asking – is that I act as a spy!"

"To put it bluntly – yes!" the Earl replied. "Now you know why I wanted somebody who speaks French as fluently as you do and will understand every word that the Marquis says to his friends without them having the slightest idea that you are eavesdropping."

Ivana realised that this could turn out to be very difficult.

Watching the expression on her face, the Earl said quietly,

"I know you are aware that this is a difficult task. If the Marquis, or any of those with whom he communicates, has any idea of what you are doing, you will undoubtedly have an unfortunate 'accident'. It will then be impossible for you to pass on any information that you have obtained on to me."

"What you are – saying is that they would – kill me!" Ivana stated.

"They will do anything to protect themselves. After what I have seen in Portugal and in France, I would not trust any Frenchman not to kill ruthlessly if his own life is at stake."

Ivana gave a little gasp, but she did not speak.

"You will understand," the Earl went on in a different tone of voice, "that the choice is yours. If you feel it is too much for you to undertake, then I promise you, Miss Sherard, I will try to find you some other post, if that is what you need and as quickly as possible."

"Of course I will do what you want of me," Ivana said rapidly.

She saw the Earl's eyes light up and then she continued,

"I feel that – Papa has brought me here – and I know that he would want me to – fight for England – as he did so valiantly himself."

"I think so too," the Earl said. "And I think it is extremely brave of you. I have to say that I never expected this very difficult and complicated position to be taken on by anyone except a man and especially one experienced in such matters."

"It may be easier because I am a woman," Ivana ventured.

The Earl looked at her and she guessed that he was thinking of something that had not come to his mind before.

"I had almost forgotten," he confessed after a moment, "that the Marquis is French. No woman looking as you do would be safe! The whole idea is ridiculous. So we must think of something else!"

Ivana gave a little cry.

"Of course not. If you are worried about me being alone with him, please may I bring my old Nanny with me wherever I am going?"

"Your *Nanny*!" the Earl exclaimed.

"She was my Nanny when I was a small baby. She has been doing the cooking since my mother remarried and we came to live in London."

"And she would come with you?" the Earl asked.

"I was going to beg whoever employed me, on my knees if necessary, to let me have Nanny with me. I know that once he finds me gone, my stepfather will not give Nanny any money and will doubtless dismiss her without a pension or reference."

"Then, of course, she must go with you," the Earl agreed. "But I am still worried, Miss Sherard. I was so intent on thinking that we must watch the Marquis in case this is some plot of Bonaparte's to insert him into our midst that I did not think of you as a beautiful young woman and therefore a temptation that no Frenchman could possibly resist."

"Nanny can look after me," Ivana replied, "and you must make it absolutely clear to the Marquis that I am just a – secretary."

She paused before she went on,

"Surely you can introduce him to a lot of the fashionable beauties who are – I am told to be found at Carlton House? In that way, as I am little – more than a – superior servant, he will not be – interested in me."

The Earl remained doubtful.

"I don't like it," he admitted. "There must be some other way around this."

"Perhaps I could make myself look old and ugly," Ivana suggested, "so that he will find me repulsive."

The Earl laughed.

"I am afraid that would be impossible, but I tell you what we will do, we will try it out while I continue to look for somebody who speaks French as well as you do."

He paused before he added in a serious voice,

"But if you find the position untenable or in any way unpleasant, then you must tell me at once. Is that a promise?"

"I promise, but I am sure if Nanny is with me, I shall be safe from any advances he might make and, if you produce a number of beautiful young ladies, I am also sure he will consider himself too grand to take any interest in a humble secretary."

The Earl doubted the logic of this, but he was in fact in a desperate position.

He had deliberately delayed the Marquis's arrival in London by arranging for him to be invited to stay at the house of an eminent Peer in Sussex.

As he had said, there were a number of people in the War Office who were prepared to trust the

Marquis. They were continually asking the Earl when the Marquis was to arrive in London and why there was a delay.

Making up his mind to take a risk, the Earl then asked her,

"How soon can you come to the house I have prepared for the Marquis? It is near here and is ready with the exception of a secretary, whom I had not found until this moment."

Ivana gave a sigh of relief.

She had been really terrified that at the very last minute the Earl might refuse to give her the position that she wanted so much.

"I can come at once, my Lord," she said. "I have only to go back with Nanny to collect our luggage."

She remembered that there would be nobody in the house as Mrs. Bell would have left there by now.

And her stepfather was not likely to return until the early hours of the morning.

Therefore she and Nanny would be on their own.

"Very well," the Earl agreed. "I will give you the address of the house and then you can go straight there."

He paused before he added,

"You realise, of course, that it would be a great mistake for me to meet you at the house or for anybody to know that you have had any communication with me?"

"But – suppose I have any information to give you?"

"I was just coming to that," the Earl smiled.

He knew as he spoke that Ivana was quick-witted. That was most certainly a point in her favour.

There might, however, be nothing for her to find out, the Earl was thinking.

In fact the Marquis de Souvenant could be of real help to the English, as he had asserted that he intended to be. Any information that he could give to the Army could help to end the War sooner than everybody hoped.

At the same time the Earl's perception told him that it had all been too easy.

He always trusted his instincts where people were concerned.

This gift had made him not only a brilliant Commander, it had also enabled him to save his men from falling into traps or being ambushed by the enemy.

What he was doing now had only the approval of Viscount Palmerston and no one else in

Government. In point of fact he had refused to discuss it with any of his colleagues thinking that it could be dangerous.

Viscount Palmerston was extremely intelligent and had agreed with him in all aspects of his mission.

"The reason that you are here, Lorimer," he had said, "is that your reports from the battlefront were so astounding that we could hardly believe them."

"That is where I would like to be now."

"I know," the Viscount replied, "but until you could return, and God knows Wellington wants you, you can be of inestimable service to us in using your brains and what you call your 'instinct'."

He glanced over his shoulder as if he thought that he was being followed before he said,

"God knows there are a great number of people here who use neither!"

The Earl laughed, but he understood exactly what Lord Palmerston was saying to him.

He had therefore decided that, where the Marquis was concerned, he would not take any chances.

He walked slowly to his desk and Ivana noticed that he had a little difficulty in sitting down.

Then he wrote on a card the address of the house where Ivana was to go.

He took a key out of the desk, saying,

"Here is the key for your own use. The servants have another one."

"You have not yet told me how I am to communicate with you, my Lord," Ivana queried.

"I have not forgotten," the Earl replied at once. "I have been working out a plan in my mind."

As he spoke, he put the key and the card down in front of Ivana.

She sat down again in the chair that she had occupied when she first arrived.

"Now listen carefully," he began. "The one thing you must never do is to come here. The Marquis must not have the slightest idea that you are in any way connected with me or with the War Office. If he should ask you how you were engaged, you must say that it was through a London Agency."

Ivana nodded.

"If you hear anything, however slight, even if it seems unimportant to you, you must make me aware of it immediately," the Earl continued.

"How do I do that?" Ivana asked him.

"I have been thinking of various different ways," he replied, "and the simplest is the best.

You will open your bedroom window and put something outside to dry in the sunshine, a handkerchief, a garment of some sort, it does not really matter, but just put it there and I shall be informed of it instantly."

"Then what happens?"

"You will go to St. James's Park, which is only a very short distance from the house in which you will be staying. In fact almost opposite Queen Anne Street, which is where the house is situated, there is a gate into the Park."

"And when I go into the Park?" Ivana enquired.

"It would be a mistake, of course, for you to leave the house while the Marquis is there. You will go alone or with your Nanny and you will find me by the canal. There is a clump of rhododendron bushes there and in front of them is a wooden seat. It is doubtful if anyone passing will notice us, but in any case we would be together for only a few minutes."

"I understand," Ivana said softly, "and, of course, I will do exactly what you tell me."

"I do not deny that you will be taking a risk if you are being watched. At the same time it is difficult to know what else we can do."

"We must just pray that no one who might be suspicious will see us," Ivana said.

"I am sure that your prayers will be answered," the Earl replied. "I am not so sure about mine."

Ivana smiled at him.

"Mama always said that all our prayers are heard and that is what I sincerely believe."

The Earl then said seriously,

"Then we can have no better protection, Miss Sherard."

Ivana picked up the card with the address written on it and then the key.

"I will go back now and start packing," she said, "then Nanny and I will drive straight to the house. When do you expect the Marquis to arrive, my Lord?"

"Now that you have been good enough to undertake this very difficult mission for me," the Earl replied, "I will arrange for him to arrive tomorrow."

Ivana stood up.

Then she said,

"You promise that, if I need you, you will come at once to the seat in the Park?"

"I will not fail you," the Earl replied answered.

He stood up from behind the desk and walked to the door with Ivana following him.

As Ivana reached the door, he held out his hand.

"I want to seriously thank you, Miss Sherard, for being extremely brave and undertaking something that I know would have made your father very proud of you."

"Wherever Papa may be, I know he will help me," Ivana replied. "All that really matters is to save many more Englishmen from losing their lives. We can do that only by beating Napoleon as quickly as possible."

"I agree with you wholeheartedly," the Earl said quietly and smiled at her.

CHAPTER THREE

The Earl held the door open and Ivana was just about to go through it when she stopped. She looked up at him and then said to him,

"Thank you again – thank you very – very much. I am so – grateful for this opportunity."

She looked so lovely as she spoke that the Earl stared at her.

Unexpectedly he pulled the door to and exclaimed,

"No! I have changed my mind!"

Ivana felt as if her heart had turned to stone.

"Ch-changed your – mind?" she stammered. "You mean – I c-cannot – help you?"

"Of course you can still help me," the Earl replied, "but in a different way."

He walked back to his desk and, sitting down, rang the bell.

Ivana followed him and her eyes looked anxious as she then sat back down on the chair that she had just risen from.

The door opened and a soldier appeared.

"Send Mr. Wilson to me immediately," the Earl ordered sharply.

"Very good, my Lord."

The soldier went away, but Ivana was looking piteously at the Earl.

"I-I don't – understand," she said. "Please – please let me do – what we – planned."

She had an idea that he was going to transfer her to some other Department and perhaps have her work for someone else.

Unexpectedly the Earl demanded,

"You did not come here alone?"

"No – as I told you, I brought my – Nanny with me," Ivana replied. "She is waiting in – a Hackney carriage which will be – very expensive."

She spoke the last words without thinking. Then she felt embarrassed in case the Earl should think that she was pleading with him for money.

At the same time she knew that every penny they possessed was precious and it would be fatal to be unnecessarily extravagant.

The Earl smiled.

"I wish to speak to your Nanny," he suggested. "Will you tell me her name?"

"It is – Miss Tate," Ivana replied. "I used her surname when I was – trying to – disguise myself because it was the – first one that came into my mind."

Before the Earl could reply, the door opened and a middle-aged man came into the room.

"You wanted me, my Lord?"

"Yes, Wilson," the Earl said. "Outside the main door you will find a Hackney carriage with a middle-aged lady inside. Her name is Miss Tate. Pay off the carriage and bring Miss Tate to me."

"Very good, my Lord."

Mr. Wilson closed the door and Ivana remarked,

"I now feel – embarrassed at having – almost asked you for money – but we really have – very little left."

"That is something which will not happen again," the Earl replied, "but, surely, Miss Sherard, you have relatives who could look after you?"

"My mother's relatives live in Cumberland," Ivana explained. "Papa's are poor and most of them have large families. They would certainly not want me."

The Earl nodded in understanding her predicament.

As there was a silence, Ivana then asked him,

"Please tell me – why you have – changed your – mind."

The Earl thought that he could tell her in only two words that she was *too beautiful*.

He had suddenly realised that it would be a crime to put her in an unprotected position as a paid servant with a Frenchman.

The Marquis would, unless he was made of stone, inevitably be attracted to her.

"I have thought of something quite different," he said aloud. "I think it will make things easier for you. I have no wish, as you are already in difficulties, to add to them."

"You are – *saving* me from – my difficulty," Ivana protested, "my stepfather must never – never find me."

The terror was back in her eyes and the Earl tried to comfort her,

"If he does, I will do my very best to rescue you. That is a promise!"

Ivana managed to smile at him.

"I hope I will never have to – keep you – to it, but it is very – reassuring to remember what you have just said to me."

The Earl felt that it was a mistake for Ivana to go on worrying.

He therefore began to talk to her about her father's Regiment and he told her just how bravely the Dragoon Guards had fought in all the battles that they had been involved in.

Ivana listened intently and she was almost disappointed when the door opened suddenly and Nanny came in.

"Ah, there you be, dearie!" she said in a tone of relief. "I was beginnin' to think I'd never find you!"

"I am afraid my office is rather a long distance from the front door," the Earl admitted apologetically.

He rose to his feet and, as Nanny came towards him, he held out his hand.

"I am delighted to meet you, Miss Tate," he started. "I need your help."

Nanny shook his hand and dropped him a little curtsey.

"I'll do whatever I can, my Lord," she said.

The Earl indicated another chair opposite his desk, as was the one that Ivana was sitting on.

Nanny was looking, Ivana thought, very respectable in her black bonnet and her black dress, which had just a touch of white at the neck.

"I want you to listen, Miss Tate," the Earl was saying slowly, "to what I propose to do with your charge, Miss Sherard."

Nanny looked a little apprehensive, but she too was listening intently.

"A short time ago the War Office," the Earl began, "at my suggestion purchased a small house in Queen Anne Street, which is only a short way from here. It belonged to Captain Ian Ashley and, when he was killed in the War, his wife begged me with tears in her eyes to buy it."

"Why did she want to sell it?" Ivana enquired.

"Because she is a Scot," the Earl explained. "She wished to return to the land of her birth with her two children."

He smiled before he added,

"It is a very expensive journey either by road or ship to Scotland. What we paid for the house and its contents not only provided her with enough for the fare but it also ensured that she did not return penniless to her own people."

"That was kind of you, my Lord," Ivana commented.

"I need not tell you," the Earl went on, "that Captain Ashley was in the Dragoon Guards just as your father was."

He must have thought that Nanny looked surprised because he added,

"Miss Sherard has already told me that you both wish to disguise yourselves. That is why I have decided you shall take over the house that was bought from Mrs. Ashley. Miss Sherard will be known as the daughter of the late Captain Ashley – 'Miss Ivana Ashley'."

Nanny gave a little exclamation of surprise, but she did not say anything.

The Earl continued,

"You will stay with her as her chaperone and it would be best if you too have a different name.

"Because Miss Ashley is hard up now that both her father and mother are gone, she has decided to take in a lodger. I am sending to her the Marquis de Souvenant in that capacity."

"So I am – not to be a – secretary!" Ivana exclaimed.

"I think it will be easier for you to do as I suggest and not become entangled with him if you are just his landlady."

Before Ivana could answer, the Earl turned to Nanny and said,

"Now you quite understand that as her chaperone, you must never leave Miss Ashley alone with the Frenchman. If he wishes to talk to her or invites her into his room, you will be present."

"I understands, my Lord," Nanny said. "It sounds very sensible to me and just what I'd expect you, as a gentleman, to arrange."

"Thank you," the Earl said. "It is the way I try to behave. I have already explained to Miss Ashley that you can never be sure of the French in war or in peace."

"That be true enough from all I hears about them Frenchies," Nanny said firmly. "You needn't worry, my Lord, about Miss Ivana. I'll take extra good care of her."

"I know you will," the Earl smiled, "and may I say that you are very like my old Nanny, who is still alive and living at my house in the country."

"I'm sure she brought your Lordship up to behave just as you should," Nanny remarked, "and that after all is what we be here for!"

The Earl laughed.

"I think you have done a very good job where Miss Ivana is concerned."

His voice changed as he then went on,

"Now, to continue. I will have you taken to the house now. Tomorrow two servants will arrive whom I have employed before and who I know are trustworthy. They are a married couple. The woman will do the cooking and clean the house and the man will act as butler and, of course, valet to the Marquis."

He paused for a deep breath before he continued,

"It would be a mistake to be too confident when you are alone. At the same time they are in the service of the War Office and their wages are paid by us."

Nanny nodded to show that she understood and the Earl went on,

"I will place the sum of two hundred pounds in the Bank nearest to here in the name of Miss Ivana Ashley."

"Two hundred – pounds?"

Ivana gasped. She could hardly believe what she had just heard.

As if she had not spoken, the Earl carried on,

"That will pay for anything in the house that you may require at the moment and for the food, which, of course, you will provide for your lodger. And every month after this, you will receive one hundred pounds, which will include the wages for Miss Tate and again the food that you will require for yourselves and the Marquis."

He thought for a moment and then added,

"I will see that a certain amount of wine is placed in the cellar. If his parties prove to be extravagant, you must let me know if you require any more and I will pay for it."

"I don't believe – it!" Ivana cried. "It all sounds too – too wonderful! Nanny has not had any – wages for – six months."

"Now, don't you worry about me, dearie, I'll be all right as long as neither of us goes hungry."

"You will not do that," the Earl said, "and understand that you are not to scrimp and save or feel too proud to spend the money on yourselves. You are doing the War Office a great service and we are quite prepared to pay for it."

"Thank you – *thank* – *you!*" Ivana enthused. "Nanny and I will be so – happy to have a – home of our own."

"We can move in at once?" Nanny asked the Earl.

Ivana knew that she was remembering that her stepfather had said that he was out for luncheon and dinner.

That meant that they had the afternoon to pack up and to move from Islington to Queen Anne Street.

"As I have said, you will have the house to yourselves for twenty-four hours," the Earl concluded. "I suggest that you make it look as much like home as possible and as if you have lived there for a long time. It is extremely important that the Marquis should not suspect that you are not who he has been told you are."

"I understand, my Lord," Nanny murmured.

The Earl was aware that Ivana was looking at him with shining eyes.

"This all – sounds too – marvellous to be – true!" she said, "but I cannot – understand why you – changed your mind, my Lord."

The Earl thought that it would undoubtedly be a mistake to tell her the truth.

Instead he replied,

"I thought the change of plan would make it easier for you to do what I have asked of you. Of course the Marquis might have found that you not as good a secretary as you were reputed to be – "

Ivana was about to protest that she thought she was very good.

Then she realised that the Earl was teasing her.

"I will just be a 'Lady of Leisure'," she said, "and do – nothing more strenuous than – arrange the flowers and water them."

"That sounds to me very sensible," the Earl remarked, "but your lodger may have other ideas. It would be helpful if he gives dinner parties and invites you to be present. Miss Tate can always, on that sort of occasion, have a headache and wish to retire early."

Ivana smiled as if she realised that he was saving her from any possible embarrassment.

"You can leave that to me, my Lord," Nanny replied. "I knows my place. At the same time I'll not have Miss Ivana gettin' into trouble such as your Lordship thinks might happen."

A look of understanding passed between them before the Earl said,

"I am now going to ask Mr. Wilson to take you to the house and, as I have already promised you, Miss Ashley, no one but Viscount Palmerston shall know that you are not the daughter of the late lamented Captain Ashley, who died fighting for his King and country."

He paused for a moment before he went on,

"Mr. Wilson will take you and Mrs. – "

The Earl stopped.

"Bell!" Nanny supplied quickly.

Ivana knew that she was using the name of their maid because it was the first one that had come into her head.

" – and Mrs. Bell," the Earl finished, "to No. 3 Queen Anne Street."

He rang for Mr. Wilson.

There was only a slight pause before the door was opened and he appeared.

"Oh, Wilson," the Earl said, "as you have sent away the Hackney carriage, will you find another or ask if there is a carriage available to take Miss Ashley and her friend to her house? It is only a short way to Queen Anne Street so, if a carriage is required, it will not be away for long."

"I'll do that, my Lord," Mr. Wilson replied.

He spoke in a way that made Ivana think that nothing he was asked to do would surprise him.

She guessed, although the Earl had not said so, that Mr. Wilson was his private secretary.

He perhaps knew a great many of the Earl's secrets and confidential affairs.

The Earl rose and held out his hand to Ivana.

"I am so glad that you came to see me," he said, "and, of course, I will send you a lodger, as you have suggested. In fact I have somebody arriving tomorrow who I think you will find is exactly the right type and who will appreciate living in a comfortable house rather than in a hotel."

"Thank you very much for helping me," Ivana replied.

She hoped that she was playing her part as well as the Earl was playing his.

The Earl shook hands with Nanny and again she bobbed him a little curtsey.

When they went to the door, Mr. Wilson walked ahead to show them the way.

Ivana found to her surprise that they did not go back along the many corridors and up and down the staircases that they had come to the Earl's study by.

Instead Mr. Wilson took them to a side door that was only a short distance away.

As they stepped outside, Ivana saw that a large number of private carriages were parked in a line.

She guessed that it was one of the reasons that the Earl had been given the study where they had been talking and so he would not have to walk very far on his injured leg.

Mr. Wilson went to the nearest carriage and spoke to the driver and he obviously agreed to do what was required of him.

Mr. Wilson opened the door and beckoned for Ivana and Nanny to climb inside.

As they did so, a footman who had been talking to another driver came hurrying to climb up onto the box.

Ivana just had time to thank Mr. Wilson for looking after them and then they drove off.

"I must say, Miss Ivana, you've landed on your feet, as you always seem to do" Nanny observed with a smile.

"That is just what I was thinking," Ivana agreed. "Oh, Nanny, my prayers have all been answered. I was so frightened, so very – very frightened that we would find nowhere to go."

"God's been very kind to us," Nanny said, "and I were prayin' too."

She sighed.

"Now all we have to do is not let God down."

"You must not forget that you are '*Mrs.* Bell'," Ivana warned with a hint of laughter in her voice.

"I shall keep on sayin' how much I miss him," Nanny said, "and that's the right word, as I've missed havin' a husband altogether!"

They both laughed.

"We have to go and pack our clothes," Ivana suggested.

"I know that," Nanny said, "but let's see what the house is like first and then we can take a Hackney carriage."

"And we can afford one with two hundred pounds in the Bank! But, Nanny, we have to travel to Islington and then back again."

Nanny did not speak, she merely opened her hand.

Ivana looked at it and saw there was a note folded several times so that it hardly covered her palm.

"What is that?" she asked.

"It's a note of ten pounds," Nanny said with awe in her voice. "As his Lordship shook my hand, I knowed he meant for me to take it. There never was a more thoughtful or kinder man!"

"He thinks of everything," Ivana agreed.

She drew in her breath and then added,

"But ten pounds, Nanny! Do be careful not to lose it."

"I wasn't born yesterday!" Nanny countered tartly.

She put the note away carefully into the pocket of her skirt.

A few minutes later they drew up outside No. 3 Queen Anne Street and Ivana opened the door with the key given to her by the Earl.

They went inside and she thought that it was a very attractive little house. It was very much the same design as the house that her mother had rented in Islington.

It was well-furnished and she could see that the pictures, mirrors and ornaments were all in their right places.

The rooms were a little stuffy because all the windows had been closed for quite some time and wooden shutters covered the large windows in the downstairs rooms.

They inspected everything in the house in detail.

Ivana knew that she and Nanny would be not only comfortable but could also make it as attractive as her home in the country had been.

She then chose the room that she wished to sleep in.

And Nanny pronounced grandly that she would have the one next door to it.

"I'm obeyin' his Lordship's wishes, Miss Ivana," she said. "I'm not lettin' you out of my sight for any reason!"

"You know I want you with me all the time, dearest Nanny," Ivana replied. "We shall be safe here – I know we will be."

She was thinking of her stepfather and Nanny replied,

"We'll put that Marquis as far away from us as we possibly can and that be at the end of the corridor."

It was a pleasant room, but not as attractive as the one that Ivana had chosen to sleep in.

For a moment she felt a little bit guilty.

Then she told herself that, if she really was the Lady of the House, she would not give up her best bedroom to a lodger, however much she wanted the money.

On the ground floor there were two very comfortable rooms. One was the drawing room and the other had been the study.

It was obvious that Ivana would keep the drawing room.

She thought, although Nanny demurred, that the Marquis should have the dining room

It was not particularly large, but it could seat at least ten people round the table easily.

"His Lordship said that the Marquis might want to give dinner parties," Ivana said. "We have no one we dare ask."

Nanny had to admit that this was true.

There was, however, another small room beside the front door.

It was not very well furnished and Ivana thought that it might have been used as a school room for children.

She thought, however, that it would be a perfect place where she and Nanny could have their meals.

"Now that we've seen everythin' except for the bedroom upstairs, where the servants'll sleep," Nanny said, "the sooner we goes back and packs up our things the better. It'll take me ages to pack up everythin' we wants."

"Yes, of course," Ivana agreed, "and I must bring all that is left of Mama's treasures, although there are now very few of them."

"You take what you wants, Miss Ivana," Nanny said firmly. "You can be quite certain if there's anythin' worth havin', Mr. Waring'll sell it."

Ivana did not answer.

She was feeling a little frightened and apprehensive.

She knew that when her stepfather found out that she had disappeared, he would be frantic in his efforts to find her.

He was really desperate for the money that Lord Hanford had promised to give him for her.

She was eager to get to Islington and the sooner they returned to the house on Queen Anne Street the better.

It flashed through her mind that perhaps her stepfather might come back unexpectedly to change for dinner.

He might even instinctively be aware that something strange was going on.

Then she told herself that she was just being imaginative. There was plenty of time. In fact there had to be time – if she and Nanny were to escape.

*

When Ivana and Nanny had arrived back at the house in Islington it was to find, as they had expected, that no one was there.

Mrs. Bell had already cleaned the kitchen and left.

Before they started to do anything, Nanny suggested having a cup of tea and insisted that Ivana should have one too. There were some shortbread biscuits to eat, which she had made the day before.

Then they both started packing. Ivana saw to her own clothes, while Nanny packed all her mother's.

The Earl had been most generous in what he was giving them and at the same time Ivana thought that it would be a great mistake to spend it too freely.

Since their engagement, if that was what it was in reality, came so easily, it might also easily come to an abrupt end.

If she discovered that the Marquis was an enemy of the British, the Earl would then want the house for somebody else.

He would certainly not continue to give them what seemed to her such an enormous sum of money.

'We must be very careful,' she told herself.

But it was just so wonderful to think that they would not go hungry.

Nor would they have to wonder, as Nanny had, whether their beds would be taken from under them to pay her stepfather's debts.

It was getting late when Nanny claimed that she could do no more.

She had packed everything that Ivana wanted to take with her.

She had also placed what food was available into a cardboard box and she had added to it the eggs that Mrs. Bell had left ready for their breakfast the following morning.

Then Nanny put into another box the tea and coffee that they had already bought to last for a whole week.

The next thing to do was to hail a Hackney carriage to take them to Queen Anne Street.

Nanny fetched one whose driver appeared to be a good-humoured man.

He exclaimed at the amount of trunks that he had to pile into the carriage as well as the cardboard boxes.

When he had finished, there was hardly room for Ivana and Nanny to squeeze inside. In fact they were both holding boxes on their knees when the carriage set off.

As they left, Ivana glanced back at the little house where her beloved mother had died.

She herself had never been happy there.

From the minute they moved in, her stepfather had begun to spend her mother's money.

All the same it had for a short time been her home. And now she was not only orphaned, but homeless.

Then she told herself that it would be ungrateful to be bitter and disillusioned.

God had looked after her and God had helped her when she least expected it. It was God she had to thank that she was not at this moment waiting terror-stricken for Lord Hanford.

They drew up outside the house on Queen Anne Street.

Although it was now growing dark, there was still a great deal to do. The beds had to be made up for one thing.

Whilst Nanny did that, Ivana hid away their trunks. The driver of the Hackney carriage had just dumped them all in the middle of the hall.

"It would be a grave mistake," she said, "if the Marquis arrived early and saw them when this is supposed to be my house."

"You're quite right, dearie," Nanny agreed. "I'll get up early tomorrow mornin'."

"I cannot believe he will arrive in time for breakfast," Ivana remarked. "At the same time I will put away what I can now."

In the end they moved everything upstairs to their rooms or else into the small room that Nanny and Ivana would use as their dining room.

"I'm too tired to unpack everything and that's the truth," Nanny grumbled.

"We will finish it all early tomorrow morning," Ivana promised her, "so go to bed now, Nanny."

"We are goin' to have somethin' to eat first," Nanny stipulated firmly.

She insisted that Ivana go downstairs with her and they sat in the kitchen and enjoyed the eggs and bacon that had Nanny cooked.

They had cups of tea, which Nanny drank at every meal.

Ivana was too tired to argue.

She merely ate everything that Nanny told her to before finally she crawled upstairs and climbed into bed.

She thought, as she snuggled down against the pillows in the comfortable bed, that her Guardian Angel was looking after her.

Also her father would most certainly approve of her trying her best to help England win the devastating War against the French

If the Marquis was really a spy and she exposed him, it would in some way be a revenge on the French for having killed him.

"I miss you, Papa – I miss you terribly!" she said aloud in the darkness. "Things were never the same after you went to fight in the War. I am sure Mama's heart died with you."

She thought of how Keith Waring had come into their lives and how he had saved her mother from her intense misery.

But he had spent all her money.

Then he had started to sell off everything that her father and mother had collected and prized over the years.

It was his insatiable and fanatical desire for more and more money that had made him agree to sell her to a cruel and wicked man.

'I hope he suffers too,' she ruminated.

It was some satisfaction to recognise that he would be distraught when he awoke in the morning to find that neither she nor Nanny were in the house.

For a moment she felt like shouting with delight because he would be so discomfited.

Then she remembered that he would not easily give up the thought of so much money.

He would search and search for her.

Lord Hanford would be looking very thoroughly for her too. He wanted her.

Despite the warmth of the bed, Ivana shivered.

She and Nanny might well have escaped for the moment but the fear of being discovered would hang over their heads like the proverbial sword of Damocles.

'Please – God, don't let them find us,' Ivana prayed.

It was a prayer that came from the very depths of her heart.

CHAPTER FOUR

Viscount Palmerston looked up from his desk as the Earl came into the room.

"Good morning, Lorimer," he greeted him, "I understand that you have heard from Lord Waterford that the Marquis wishes to come straight here."

"He wishes to see you," the Earl replied, "and he is very determined to make himself of importance."

The Viscount laughed.

"Are you already using your perception," he enquired, "for which, I may say, I have the highest regard."

"I hope so," the Earl smiled, "but, of course, I may well be wrong. He may be a real ally and not just trying to impress us."

"The information that we received from him last month was in fact of considerable use to the Duke of Wellington," the Viscount Palmerston pointed out.

"There was not much of it," the Earl remarked somewhat scathingly.

"If he is indeed a wolf disguised as a sheep," the Viscount went on, "I am relying on you, Lorimer, to exercise your usual brilliance at finding out the truth."

The Earl made a gesture with his hand. Then, because his leg was hurting him, he sat down in front of the Viscount's desk.

"We must be very careful," he said reflectively, "not to let this Frenchman have any idea that Miss Sherard is not who she pretends to be."

"You have already impressed that on me," the Viscount replied. "I assure you, Lorimer, I can be very discreet when the occasion demands it."

The Earl laughed.

"You are well aware that I respect your discretion in every possible way except where a pretty woman is concerned."

The Viscount, who was a well-known womaniser, laughed.

"I take that as a compliment. Otherwise, I assure you, I would make you pay for it in one way or another."

They were both laughing when the door opened and a senior servant announced,

"*Monsieur le Marquis de Souvenant!*"

As the Frenchman came into the room, the Viscount quickly rose to his feet and the Earl did the same but more slowly.

He was, the Earl thought, exactly what he had expected, a middle-aged man, slim, alert-looking and well dressed.

He did not look like a man who had suffered in any way from his imprisonment.

The Viscount walked forward, holding out his hand.

"Welcome to England, *monsieur*," he began. "And, needless to say, I am delighted to meet you."

"I am charmed to be here," the Marquis answered in excellent English.

As he continued to talk, the Earl realised that, while he had a slight accent, he had no difficulty with the language.

"I cannot tell you what it means," he was saying to the Viscount, "to be free and to be with people who wish, as I do, to be rid of this Corsican upstart who has plunged my country into complete chaos."

"I know how you must feel," the Viscount said sympathetically. "May I introduce the Earl of Lorimer, who, having been wounded, is currently on leave from the battlefront."

The Marquis turned to the Earl and held out his hand.

"My commiserations, *monsieur*," he said. "I can only hope that your wound will soon be healed."

"That is what I am hoping myself," the Earl replied, "and may I as well welcome you to England."

The Marquis acknowledged his words with a nod of his head and the Earl turned to the Viscount,

"I will leave you now, my Lord. I am going to the country for a few days where there are matters on my estate that require my attention."

"I shall miss you," the Viscount said genially, "but, of course, you will be back in time for the Prince Regent's party next week?"

"I hope so – " the Earl began to say.

"Is His Royal Highness giving a party?" the Marquis interposed. "If so, that is something I should enjoy attending more than anything else. I can assure you, *monsieur*, that tales of the superb hospitality at Carlton House have not only reached Paris but are to my countrymen a continual source of envy, hatred and malice!"

Both Englishmen laughed at this and the Marquis went on,

"If you could get me an invitation, I should be so very grateful, not only as a curiosity-seeker, but also because I shall have a chance of meeting many of my own kin who have been living in England since the Revolution and who I know have been befriended by His Royal Highness."

"But, of course you must be present," the Viscount said. "So I will speak to His Royal Highness about it at the first opportunity."

"*Merci, merci*," the Marquis sighed. "That will be something I shall look forward to with great anticipation."

The Earl walked to the door. He somewhat exaggerated his limp as he did so.

When he was outside in the corridor, he heard the Marquis saying,

"What a charming man! I am sorry he was so badly wounded."

"It is a tragedy," the Viscount replied, "because he is irreplaceable to the Army."

The Earl did not wait to hear any more. There was, however, an expression on his face as he walked down the corridor that Viscount Palmerston would have understood.

*

The following morning Nanny came into breakfast in the small room that Ivana and she were using for their meals.

"Our lodger's determined to sleep late," she said. "There's a note outside his door sayin' he doesn't want to be called."

"It was after two o'clock when he came in," Ivana replied.

"Why were you awake at that hour, I'd like to know?" Nanny asked her.

"I found it difficult to sleep because I had so much – to think about," Ivana answered.

She lowered her voice as she added,

"I have found a way by which I can hear exactly what is said in the study."

"Have you indeed!" Nanny exclaimed. "What's that?"

"You know in the drawing room the fireplace backs onto the one in the study."

Nanny nodded and Ivana went on,

"Either Mrs. Ashley or else the person who designed the house, has scooped out the wall on either side of both fireplaces so that there are shelves on which stand china ornaments and books in the study."

Nanny was listening, but there was a puzzled expression in her eyes that showed Ivana that she did not really understand.

"Do you not see, Nanny, that there is only a thin partition between the two rooms? When you were talking to Mrs. Smith, the housekeeper, yesterday, I could hear everything that you were saying."

"That's useful," Nanny remarked. "Equally I don't like you bein' involved in this sort of thing, however kind his Lordship might have been to us."

"He would not have been kind if he had not thought I spoke perfect French and would, therefore, understand what the Marquis said to anyone of his own nationality who calls here to see him."

"He seems a decent enough sort of man," Nanny said reflectively, "not that I would trust him!"

Ivana did not reply.

Although she thought that it would be a mistake to say so to Nanny, there was something she did not like about the Marquis.

He had been very effusive when he had arrived the previous night.

He expressed his gratitude very volubly that she should allow him to lodge in her house.

"The Viscount Palmerston," he said, "has told me how kind you have been in saying I could stay with you. I will be far more comfortable staying here than in a hotel. *Merci, merci, mademoiselle*, I am deeply in your debt."

Ivana smiled at him.

She then said that she was so delighted to be of any assistance to Viscount Palmerston, whom she greatly admired.

She wondered if the Marquis had met the Earl, but knew that it would be a mistake for her to ask questions.

All she had to do now was to carry out the Earl's instructions and watch her lodger, besides, of course, listening for anything he might say that would interest the War Office.

The Marquis did not appear downstairs until it was nearly luncheontime.

He had sent a message by Smith to say that he would be in to luncheon and he hoped that Miss Ashley would honour him by being his guest.

Ivana sent back a message to say that she and Mrs. Bell would be delighted to accept his kind invitation.

She wondered what the Marquis would make of Nanny.

She had been busy in the morning finding things that Nanny could wear that would make her look more like a chaperone.

Fortunately there was one black gown that had belonged to her mother that had always been too big for her.

There was also a bonnet trimmed with black plumes, which Mrs. Sherard had worn at a funeral.

"It is easier for you to be in mourning, as your own gown is black," Ivana remarked, "and so there is no reason for the Marquis to see you in the cotton dresses you wear in the mornings."

"I'll be ever so grand, I just won't know meself!" Nanny exclaimed. "But his Lordship's right. You must have a chaperone seein' how young and pretty you are."

"Thank you, Nanny," Ivana laughed, "but I would doubt if the Marquis will find it easy to compliment me with you scowling at him."

They had luncheon in the dining room.

The Marquis managed to compliment her several times, but in a manner that was not in the least embarrassing.

In fact Ivana had a distinct impression that his mind was on matters other than her.

She told herself that the Earl need not worry, the Marquis had other things to occupy his brain and was not in the slightest interested in women.

After luncheon the Marquis left the house and Ivana rearranged one of the rooms.

She soon found that time was rather heavy on her hands.

She thought it would be interesting to talk to the Earl but had no excuse for doing so.

The day passed slowly with Nanny busy making her own black gown look a little more elaborate.

She was also beginning to feel a bit bored as there was so little to do.

The Smiths were most efficient in performing their duties and, when Ivana and Nanny dined alone, the food was delicious.

Nanny retired to her bed early and Ivana was just about to undress when she heard the front door opening and the Marquis was returning.

He was not alone, for she heard them talking as they went into the study.

For a moment she hesitated, thinking it would be unnecessary to spy on him so soon in his stay at the house.

Then she told herself that she had been given a task to do and, when the Earl had been so kind to her, she should not be lazy.

She therefore crept down the stairs and tiptoed into the drawing room.

Quietly she closed the door and then moved across the room, guided by the light coming in through the window.

She reached the mantelpiece and moved to the side where there were pieces of china.

She had already carefully moved a number of books from the shelf in the study.

Because they were heavy and covered with leather, she had replaced them with smaller volumes, which were lighter and did not completely fill the shelves.

Standing in the darkness of the drawing room, Ivana heard the Marquis saying in French,

"I cannot tell you what a relief it is to have come here without any trouble."

"I thought you would manage it, Louis," the other man said. "No one could be cleverer than you when you want your own way."

"I would certainly hope so," the Marquis replied. "I have a great deal to do as you can readily imagine."

"When is Pier arriving?" the other Frenchman asked him.

"Tomorrow or the next day. You know it is not easy to bribe the smugglers."

"Why not, when always they want more money?" the visitor enquired.

The Marquis lowered his voice.

"They take money from us and are delighted to do so if there is room in their boat. At the same time there is always the risk that, just as soon as you set foot on English soil, they will denounce you."

"I see what you mean," his visitor said. "Thank God, I had no difficulty of that sort."

"You were fortunate," the Marquis commented dryly.

There was silence for a moment.

Then the Marquis said,

"I shall be informed when Pier arrives."

"I will be leaving now," his friend said. "You will let me know when Pier gets in touch with you. I suppose he knows where to find you?"

"Of course," the Marquis responded sharply. "I have made every possible arrangement of that sort."

"I just thought you would. There is no one more efficient than you are, Louis, when you have work to do."

"I most certainly have no intention," the Marquis said, "of making a mistake where this mission is concerned."

As he had been talking, he must have opened the door and walked out for his voice faded away.

Ivana was then aware that he and the visitor were moving down the passage towards the front door.

She did not dare move.

She held her breath as she heard him saying 'goodbye' and the Marquis then closed the door quietly behind him.

She was wondering frantically what she should say to him if by any chance he came into the drawing room.

To her relief, however, she heard him walk back down the passage and go into the study.

Walking on tiptoe, she crossed the drawing room and then ran up the stairs.

Only when she reached her own bedroom did she wonder if anything had been said that could be of any possible interest to the Earl.

He had said, of course, that he wanted to know everything however unimportant it might appear to her.

Perhaps the arrival of Pier was important, she did not know, but obviously she must tell him.

Remembering his instructions for her, she went to a drawer and brought out a large white handkerchief.

It was a warm night and her window was open.

She spread the handkerchief over the windowsill just as the Earl had instructed her to do.

If whoever was watching did not see it tonight, he would certainly see it first thing in the morning.

She undressed and then climbed wearily into bed.

*

It was after breakfast the next morning that Ivana slipped out of the house while Nanny was tidying her bedroom.

It was not yet nine o'clock.

The Marquis had left instructions that he was not to be called until nine-thirty.

Ivana felt quite safe in going alone into the Park and the Earl had made it very clear that she was to come alone.

She found the canal and then the part where there was a little bridge across it.

On the other side of the canal she saw the clumps of bushes where she thought that the wooden seat would be concealed.

As she moved past some rhododendrons, she saw that the seat was occupied and on it was the Earl.

She gave a little murmur of surprise, then hurried towards him.

He did not rise, his bad leg was stretched out in front of him. Instead he put out his hand and drew her down beside him on the seat.

"You are here so early!" Ivana exclaimed. "I thought that I would have to wait for you, my Lord."

"I told you I would come at once when you sent for me," he answered, "and here I am."

"What I have to tell you is not very much," Ivana started apologetically, "but you told me to tell you everything that occurred, however inconsequential it might seem."

"That is what I told you," the Earl said, "and I am very grateful that you have obeyed my orders."

Ivana smiled at him.

Although she was not aware of it, she was looking very lovely in a chip straw bonnet trimmed with wild flowers.

It had been one of her mother's favourites and she had put it on, not because she thought the Earl would admire it, but because her mother had liked it so much.

"Now what have you to tell me?" the Earl prompted her.

Ivana had a very good memory.

Her father had encouraged her when she was small to learn the Collects in the Prayer Book by heart every Sunday and she had learnt all the poems that he read to her so that she could repeat them to her mother.

Her father had also played a game of saying things to her and then testing her to see if she could repeat them word for word.

Ivana found all this particularly useful now.

She told the Earl exactly what the Marquis had said to his visitor and what the man had replied.

The Earl listened attentively not missing a word of what she was telling him.

When she finished and he did not say anything, she added a little apologetically,

"It does not sound very important. Was I right to send for you to come here?"

"Absolutely right!" he replied. "In fact what you have told me is of great value."

He saw the question in her eyes and added,

"Perhaps not immediately, but it is like writing a book. Every chapter leads to something else, perhaps to a denouement, perhaps to a drama, a murder or even a Wedding."

Ivana chuckled.

"If you can make a whole book out of what I tell you, it will certainly be exciting!"

"That is what I am hoping," the Earl said quietly.

There was a silence before Ivana said hesitatingly,

"Do you – really think – he is a – spy?"

The Earl spread out his hands.

"I don't know. Neither of us knows, Ivana, and that is what we have to find out."

Ivana realised that he had now called her by her Christian name for the first time and so she said,

"You are paying me a very – great compliment in letting me think I am – important to you if to – nobody else."

"I am sure that there are other people who you are important to as well," the Earl replied.

He was just speaking politely and Ivana, however, had a sudden picture of Lord Hanford and her stepfather searching for her.

The fear was back in her eyes.

"It's all right," the Earl said quietly. "You are quite safe."

"How can I be – sure?" Ivana asked. "They will be – looking for – me."

"How is it possible for him to find you?" the Earl asked reasonably. "After all you have changed your name and your address. The only other person who knows where you are, apart from myself, is Viscount Palmerston."

Ivana gave a sigh.

"You are right – of course. It was – stupid of me to be – frightened and I can only say – again how – grateful I am for your – kindness."

"Indeed I am very grateful to you for what you are doing for me," the Earl said. "So we can call it quits and stop being humble to each other."

Ivana laughed at that.

"I cannot imagine you, my Lord, being humble to anyone!"

"I assure you, it is what I have had to be at times in my life," the Earl answered, "and it is not something I enjoy under any circumstances."

Ivana thought that he was so authoritative and so prestigious that she could not imagine him kowtowing to anybody.

He rose to his feet.

"Thank you," he said. "Please let me know exactly what happens on every day and, if necessary, on every hour. I would not ask you if it was not of the utmost importance both to me and, of course, to our country."

Ivana smiled at him.

"Now, we must not leave together," the Earl went on, "so I will walk slowly back the way I have come and, when I am out of sight, you then go back to the house and tell Nanny to look after you."

"She is doing that very well," Ivana replied.

The Earl did not say anything more. He walked away.

Ivana thought, watching him, that his limp was a little better than it had been the day she first met him.

'If it gets completely better,' she thought, 'then he will go back to France.'

She knew without being told that, as a soldier, he would rather be at the battlefront and not scheming secretly as he was now behind closed doors.

'He is so strong, so handsome and so clever,' she told herself.

As she walked back, she continued thinking about the Earl.

She so wished that he would tell her more of what he did and also of what made him suspicious of the Marquis.

*

The next day nothing happened, nor the next.

The Marquis came and went and, when he was in the house, he was usually shut away in his own sitting room.

Ivana thought that he might be reading, writing or perhaps just sleeping in an armchair.

Then on the third day the invitations began to arrive.

After Smith had taken them in at the front door from either a postman or a groom, he put them on the table in the hall.

It gave Ivana a chance to look at them before the Marquis returned to the house and took them into his study.

It was not difficult to guess those that were private invitations from London hostesses.

The Marquis placed them on the mantelpiece in his study and she recognised some of the names of *émigrés*, who had come from France during the Revolution and had then settled in various parts of England.

She had read their names in the Social columns of *The Morning Post*, which her father and mother took in preference to other London newspapers.

There were always lists of the guests who had appeared at parties at Carlton House and the other great houses of the City.

Parties given by the Duke of Devonshire, the Duke and Duchess of Bedford and the Countess of Bessborough.

Ivana had read of their names with considerable interest.

When they moved to London, she thought it would be fascinating to see these famous people driving in the Park.

Unfortunately Islington was rather too far from Hyde Park and Nanny could not always spare the time to accompany her to Rotten Row.

Ivana knew that this was where most of the beautiful ladies and famous gentlemen of London would be parading in the morning either on horseback or in open carriages.

Nevertheless she knew the names of some of the French aristocrats and she noted that they at least had accepted the Marquis as one of themselves.

She thought that this piece of information might well be of interest to the Earl again.

But, as there was nothing else, she thought that she should wait.

She decided that there must be something more important or unusual to relate before she alerted the Earl.

The following evening, she and Nanny dined with the Marquis.

After dinner he came into the drawing room and sat talking with them.

He made it obvious, without actually saying so, that he wished to talk alone with Ivana.

Nanny, however, made it quite clear that she had absolutely no intention of leaving Ivana unchaperoned in the drawing room or anywhere else for that matter.

Finally, after paying her some fulsome compliments and trying to speak in such a low voice that Nanny could not hear him, the Marquis went to his study.

As soon as he had gone, Nanny exclaimed,

"Now at last we can go to bed! If he takes any more liberties with you, I'll give him a good piece of my mind!"

"Please, Nanny, don't make any trouble," Ivana begged her. "It is just the French way of talking, which is so different from the English."

"Whatever way it is, I don't like it," Nanny persisted. "And the next time he invites us, we'll say we've got another engagement!"

Ivana laughed.

"He will know that is untrue."

"There'll be nothin' he can do about it and that's for sure," Nanny replied. "Now off to bed with you, Miss Ivana, and make sure of your beauty sleep."

"What do I need so much beauty for?" Ivana asked provocatively. "You know as well as I do that we dare not invite anybody to the house or let them know where we are."

"And a good thing too, if you asks me," Nanny said, "otherwise you can be quite certain your stepfather and that horrible friend of his will be hammerin' on the door before you can say 'Jack Robinson'!"

Ivana cried in horror and Nanny added for good measure,

"Just you start countin' your blessings. The biggest blessin' we've got is to have dropped in here and them as wishes us no good has no idea where we be."

Ivana kissed her.

"You are quite right, Nanny, I am being very ungrateful, but there does seem to be very little for us to do when we have always been so busy."

Nanny did not say anything more, she merely left the drawing room and went upstairs.

Ivana was looking for a book that she had started reading that afternoon when she heard a knock on the front door.

Nobody appeared to be answering it and there came another impatient *rat-tat*.

Then she heard Smith's footsteps coming from the kitchen.

Ivana waited in the drawing room. The door was slightly ajar and she heard Smith open the front door.

"I wish see Monsieur le Marquis," she heard a voice say.

He obviously had a strong French accent.

"Is Monsieur expectin' you?" Smith asked.

"*Oui, oui*, 'e expect me," the caller snapped back impatiently.

"Then come this way, sir, if you please," Smith said as he walked slowly across the hall.

Ivana heard footsteps following him before the visitor was shown into the study.

As soon as the door had closed behind him, she shut the drawing room door.

Then she went as quietly as she could to the mantelpiece.

The Marquis must have been sitting waiting for his visitor, because she then heard him exclaim in French,

"Pier! Is it really you?"

"I am here, *monsieur*, and very lucky to have managed it."

"You had difficulties?"

"Yes, but I was able to overcome them and I managed to get to London without any further hindrance."

"There has not been trouble?" the Marquis asked with an anxious note in his voice.

"I don't know what you call 'trouble'," his guest replied, "but you can give me a drink as I need it!"

The Marquis went to the grog tray that stood in the far corner of the room.

Ivana heard him pour something into a glass before he asked,

"You had better tell me what happened."

"I was accused of being the enemy by some idiot Englishman," Pier replied.

He did not say anything more.

"You mean – you killed him?" the Marquis questioned.

"I disposed of him and threw his body into the sea," Pier replied, "and that is the right place for it!"

"Thank God you came here safely!" the Marquis exclaimed. "We have a lot of planning to work on."

"I thought that was what you would say," Pier answered.

He was obviously drinking and enjoying whatever the Marquis had handed him, because there was silence for a few minutes before he exclaimed,

"That was good! And you can give me another."

Ivana heard the Marquis move across to the grog tray once again.

As he walked back with the glass, he said to Pier,

"You are quite certain that no one knows you are here?"

"Not unless they are a bird in the sky or a snake on the ground!" Pier replied flippantly.

"Then I have everything set for what we talked about in Paris," the Marquis answered. "It was just by good fortune that I received this."

Ivana thought that he then must have put something into Pier's hand.

There was silence while he read whatever it was.

Then he exclaimed,

"You are very clever! Even cleverer than I gave you credit for."

"That is what I thought myself," the Marquis answered, "and now all we have to do is to go over in detail what I have planned, step by step, until it is absolutely impossible for you to make any mistakes."

"That is what we will do," Pier agreed, "but for now I need a bed for the night and it had better be a comfortable one."

"It would be a considerable mistake for you to stay here," the Marquis answered. "I have arranged accommodation for you in a respectable and decent lodging house. It is kept by an elderly couple and I told them you are employed by the Countess of Onslow, who is a friend of His Royal Highness the Prince Regent."

"So I am going up in the Social scale," Pier observed in an amused voice.

"They are simple folk and will not have the least suspicion that I have not told them the truth."

"Good! Now tell me where this place is and tomorrow we will discuss, as you say, your plan, so that I don't put a foot wrong."

"I know you will not fail me or the man we serve," the Marquis exhorted him.

Pier did not answer because he was obviously still drinking.

Then he said in a thick voice,

"I shall be off now, Come and show me where this place is."

"Of course," the Marquis answered. "I will introduce you formally and don't forget your manners! The *émigrés* have ingratiated themselves with the English and given themselves a lot of airs and graces,"

"Who would not in the circumstances?" Pier asked.

He must have then risen to his feet and walked to the door.

Ivana heard them cross the hall and leave the room. She knew that the Marquis had a key that he could let himself in with.

When they had gone, she ran up the stairs. At least now, she thought, she had something of particular interest to relay to the Earl.

When she climbed into bed, she felt glad not only because she was being of use but also because she would see him again.

'I want to see him again,' she thought. 'He is the most interesting man I have ever met.'

As she fell asleep, she was still thinking of him.

CHAPTER FIVE

"That was really wonderful!" Ivana enthused.

"I do agree with you," Nanny replied. "Those young boys sang like angels and that's a fact!"

They were walking back to the house from Westminster Abbey.

They had heard the choir from the Abbey and from two other Churches rehearsing for a concert.

It was the Earl who had sent them the tickets with a note saying,

"I think you will enjoy this."

There was no signature, but Ivana knew at once that it was from him.

Ivana was thrilled at the idea of hearing the choirs of the three Churches, which were to sing at Canterbury Cathedral in a week's time.

She had been feeling slightly apprehensive that there might be people there who would notice her.

And perhaps they would say something afterwards that would give her stepfather a clue as to where she was.

When she and Nanny entered Westminster Abbey, they found that their seats were in the far side of the Nave.

Looking round Ivana realised that the congregation consisted mostly of elderly people and she thought too that the majority of them were not the sort of people who would associate with the raffish set that entertained and amused her stepfather.

Once she felt reassured, she settled down to enjoy the singing.

It was, as Nanny had agreed, absolutely wonderful.

The young clear voices soared up to the roof and to Ivana they seemed to be part of the stained-glass windows, the flowers on the Altar and the sanctity of the Abbey itself.

The event had begun with prayers led by the Bishop of London.

Ivana prayed fervently that she would be able to help the Earl and not disappoint him.

When they came out of Westminster Abbey, it was growing dark and luckily they had only a short distance to walk back to Queen Anne Street.

Because they had not taken a key with them, Ivana raised the knocker.

The door was opened by Smith and, as they walked in, he informed her,

"Monsieur's back, miss, and with a friend in the study."

Ivana felt guilty, she should have been on duty and attentive. Perhaps she had missed hearing something vital that would be of great interest to the Earl.

As Smith disappeared back into the kitchen, she took off her bonnet and handed it to Nanny. She then took off the wrap that she had taken with her in case it was cold.

Nanny did not say anything.

Ivana realised, however, as she went up the stairs, that she disliked and disapproved of what she was doing.

She went into the drawing room, which was in darkness.

There was just a faint light coming from a street lamp a little farther down the road.

She tiptoed up to the mantelpiece.

Immediately she heard the voice of a man talking in the study.

It was the Marquis, who was speaking in French.

" – by the garden door," he was saying.

"*Oui*, I have found out where it is."

She knew at once that the answer came from Pier.

Then the Marquis dropped his voice to a whisper as he said something that sounded to Ivana like,

" – a Field Marshal."

In an effort to hear a little more clearly, Ivana then bent her head closer to the shelf.

In doing so she knocked over one of the ornaments.

It fell to the ground with a bang.

As she reached out her hand to pick it up, the Marquis asked Pier sharply,

"What was that?"

"I heard nothing," Pier replied.

"Well, I did," the Marquis said. "I had better investigate."

A feeling of horror swept over Ivana as she realised what a dangerous position she was now in.

The Earl had indeed warned her.

But she had tried not to think about what would happen if she was discovered.

She heard footsteps going across the room before the study door was opened.

Frantically she ran to the other end of the drawing room and threw herself down behind the sofa.

It was a piece of Louis XV furniture with a gilded back, arms and legs. It was covered with blue damask, the same colour and material as the curtains.

Desperately Ivana squeezed herself under it, still holding the china ornament against her breast.

She heard the door open.

As the Marquis came into the room, she realised that he must have stopped in the hall to pick up one of the candles that stood on the side table.

As he stood still, looking round, she remembered that her face would show up white in the darkness.

She hid it in her folded arms, which meant that she could not see anything.

She was aware, however, that the Marquis had walked over to the mantelpiece and he was examining the shelves on either side of it.

It was then she thought that only her Guardian Angel could have prompted her to bring the ornament with her.

There was nothing to explain to the Marquis the reason for the sound that he had heard.

Ivana was aware that if he searched and found her, it was doubtful that she would live for very much longer.

She prayed frantically for help.

'Save me – *God* – *please save* – *me*!' she entreated God in her heart.

At the same time she was thinking that if she was discovered, the only person who could save her was the Earl.

The Marquis spent some time at the fireplace and then he moved into the centre of the room.

He lifted the candle and held it high above his head.

Fortunately Ivana had gone to Church in the plainest gown she possessed, which was of deep blue.

She knew that unless the Marquis came closer to the sofa, he would not be aware that she was beneath it.

He was, however, still looking round the room in every direction.

Her heart was beating so frantically that she was sure he would hear it.

She prayed and prayed and went on praying.

Then, at long last, as if he was satisfied that what he had heard could not have been of any significance, he went from the drawing room and closed the door behind him.

Ivana did not move.

She remembered reading in a book that had amused her and her father how criminals were often caught. Thinking that whoever was looking for them had left the room, they came out from their hiding place only to discover that whoever was looking for them was there waiting to arrest them.

She did not move, she hardly breathed.

Then, to her utter relief, she heard the door of the study close.

Very very softly there came the sound of the two men talking again.

Because she was feeling so frightened, she could not wait to listen to anything more that was said.

Terrified in case she should upset anything else, she made her way carefully to the door.

Before she opened it, she took off her shoes.

Carrying them she slipped across the hall and up the stairs. Although she was not aware of it, the colour was coming back into her cheeks.

She put the china ornament she held in one hand on the mantelpiece and asked herself how she could have been so stupid as to knock it over.

'Now he will be suspicious,' she thought.

She was sure that the Marquis would be watching her. If so how could she go on spying on him?

'I must tell the Earl how foolish I have been,' she decided.

Going to the window she looked out and saw the stars twinkling up in the sky and a full moon was creeping up over the roofs of the houses.

'How can I have been so careless?' she asked the Heavens over and over again.

There was no answer.

Before she got into her bed, Ivana put a white handkerchief on her windowsill and made certain that it was held firmly in place by a book.

It was something that she had not thought of before.

But, if the wind swept it away during the night, then the Earl would not be waiting for her in the Park.

Because she was still so upset and frightened, she found it quite impossible to sleep.

Instead she tossed and turned, feeling as if everything had been changed by one careless slip.

If she was no longer of any use to the Earl, he might ask her and Nanny to leave and put somebody else more competent in their place.

'We – must stay – we must,' she thought despairingly, 'otherwise we shall have to find cheaper lodgings and Step-Papa – may be searching them and find me!'

So many problems seemed to appear all because she had so carelessly knocked over one small china ornament.

Finally, just before dawn, she fell asleep at last.

*

It was two hours later that Ivana awoke and knew that she must now go to the Park.

She told Nanny where she was going. She then sniffed disapprovingly, but did not try to prevent her from her intention.

"Just you come back quick as you can," Nanny urged sharply. "I don't like you walkin' about the streets by yourself. It's just not right."

"It is just a short distance, Nanny," Ivana said soothingly. "I shall be back long before Monsieur is awake and requires his breakfast."

Nanny did not say anything more and Ivana hurried down the stairs and let herself out onto the street.

She reached the Park and breathed in volumes of fresh air that she was certainly needing after last night.

As it was still so early in the morning, she was not really surprised to find that the Earl was not there waiting for her.

She sat down on the wooden seat, twisting her fingers because she was feeling agitated.

She wondered if the Earl would be angry with her.

When at last he came walking through the bushes, she jumped to her feet.

"You have – come! *You have – come!*" she cried as if she had been afraid that he would not do so.

He looked at her searchingly.

Then, as he sat down on the wooden seat, he asked quietly,

"What has happened to upset you?"

Ivana drew in her breath.

"I have – done something – very stupid," she answered, "and I am – afraid you will be angry with me!"

The Earl put out his hand and laid it over hers. He realised that she was trembling and her fingers were very cold.

"Tell me what has happened," he suggested. "I promise you, whatever it is, I will not be angry with you."

"I-I have done – something so – foolish," Ivana admitted, "that I am – ashamed to tell you – how idiotic I have been."

The Earl's fingers tightened on hers.

She thought, because his fingers were warm and strong, that it was very comforting.

"Tell me what you have done," he coaxed her, "and stop being afraid of me."

"You are – a very frightening – person," Ivana pointed out.

The Earl smiled.

"I try not to be."

"I want to be – as clever as you – are but, of course, it is impossible."

"Now you are flattering me," the Earl said. "And I can tell you, without any flattery, that I think you are one of the most intelligent women I have ever met."

"Y-you will not – think so," Ivana sighed, "when you – hear what I have d-done."

"What have you done?" he enquired.

"When we came – back from Westminster Abbey – last night," Ivana began, "and thank you for – sending us the tickets for the concert – "

"I thought you would enjoy it," the Earl said.

"It was wonderful – so wonderful and, as Nanny said, the choirboys sang like angels."

The Earl smiled, but he did not interrupt her as Ivana went on,

"When we arrived back – Smith opened the door and told us that – the Marquis was in the study with a friend."

"Did you know who it was?" the Earl asked.

"Not at first," Ivana answered, "but – when Smith had gone back to the kitchen – I gave Nanny my bonnet and hurried into the – drawing room."

Ivana paused for a moment before she continued,

"The minute I – heard the men speaking – I knew that it was Pier who was – with him."

"What did they say which made you realise that?" the Earl queried.

"They were talking in very low voices," Ivana said, "and I just heard the Marquis say, ' – by the garden door' and Pier replied that he knew – where that was."

Again she paused for a moment because her words seemed to be falling over themselves before she continued,

"The Marquis said in – a whisper – something that sounded like – 'a Field Marshal' and it was – then that something – terrible happened."

"What was it?" the Earl asked sharply.

"In my – effort to get nearer – to the wall – I knocked one of the – china ornaments off the shelf."

The Earl did not speak aa Ivana went on,

"Forgive me – please forgive me for – being so careless – and stupid. I am very sorry – so terribly sorry."

"What happened after that?" the Earl queried.

"The Marquis asked, 'what was that?' and I – realised that he was coming – into the – drawing room."

"He found you?"

"Oh, no – I was so – afraid he might, but I ran – across the room and then – hid under – the sofa."

Ivana tried to steady her voice as she carried on with her story,

"I just had time – because he stopped to pick up a candle in the h-hall."

"Then what happened?" the Earl prompted.

"The Marquis looked at the shelves on – either side of the mantelpiece – for some time – and then he looked – around the room."

"But he did not discover you?"

"N-no."

The Earl breathed a sigh of relief.

"Thank God for that!"

There were tears in Ivana's eyes as she looked up at him.

"I – know how – stupid I have been. Now that – he is suspicious – perhaps you – will send me away – and bring in someone b-better."

The Earl's fingers once again tightened on hers.

"Now, listen to me," he said. "You have done an excellent job and told me all I wanted to know."

Ivana stared at him.

"How – how can I have – done that when I have – been so st – "

"I want you to stop worrying," the Earl interrupted, "and ask me no questions. Later I will explain to you in detail exactly how brilliant you have been, but for the moment I want you just to obey me."

"You know – I will, my Lord," Ivana murmured.

"Then go back to the house right now. Stay with Nanny and see as little as possible of the Marquis"

"D-do you mean – I don't have to – spy on him anymore?"

The Earl shook his head.

"You have done all that I asked of you. Now just behave like the Lady of the House and try to enjoy yourself," the Earl urged. "I am not angry with you, not in the slightest. Just very very grateful."

"But – I-I don't understand."

"There is no reason for you to understand anything. Just trust me. Very shortly I hope to be able to tell you just how clever you have been."

"I-I just feel – ashamed of – myself," Ivana murmured.

"I, on the contrary, am very proud of you," the Earl reassured her.

"You are – really? You are not – just saying – that to make me – feel happier?"

"When you know me better," the Earl replied, "you will know that I always say what I think and never, if at all possible, tell a lie."

"I know – that without you – telling me," Ivana answered.

"Then you must believe me when I tell you that you have been of inestimable help and, as soon as it is possible, I will explain everything that puzzles you at the moment."

There was silence and then Ivana asked, looking up at him,

"And you – do not wish – Nanny and me to – leave the – house?"

"Certainly not," the Earl replied. "Because I know that you will carry out my instructions

~126~

exactly as I wish you to do. I want you to behave quite naturally and certainly not look as worried as you did when I arrived just now."

"I was worried, desperately worried, in case you were angry and – sent us away."

"Now I want you to look happy and, of course, beautiful," the Earl said quietly.

Ivana looked up at him in surprise.

For a moment their eyes met and she felt that it was just impossible to look away.

Then he took his hand from hers and rose to his feet.

"Go back to Nanny," he suggested. "I am going to Regent's Park and afterwards I have to go to the country. If I cannot see you for two or three days, please don't be worried."

"You mean – I am not to put out – a handkerchief if I have – something to tell you?" Ivana asked.

"You will have no need to tell me anything," the Earl replied, "except that you are happy and safe. You now have no further need to watch the Marquis or listen to what he says."

Ivana, who was still sitting on the seat, stared up at him.

It all seemed incomprehensible and puzzling.

At the same time the Earl was smiling at her and she felt as if the sun had suddenly come out.

"Thank you, Ivana," he said quietly, "and remember, I am very proud of you."

He rose from the wooden seat and then walked away.

Once he had gone Ivana put her hands up to her eyes.

She could hardly believe that he had behaved so differently towards her from what she had expected.

Now she need no longer be afraid of being sent away or that the Earl was angry with her for what she had done.

'I don't – understand what is – happening,' she told herself, 'but why should I worry – when everything now seems all right?'

She waited for a few more minutes and then walked back to Queen Anne Street feeling as if she had wings on her heels.

As soon as she entered the house, she ran upstairs to Nanny, who was busy tidying her bedroom.

She flung herself against her, saying,

"It's all right, Nanny! Perfectly all right! The Earl is not angry with me."

"Why should he be?" Nanny enquired.

Ivana then remembered that she had not told Nanny why she was upset and what had happened the previous night.

She certainly did not wish to repeat how stupid she had been.

"I thought," she said after a moment as Nanny was waiting for an answer, "that he might be – angry because I had given him so – little information, but he says that he is satisfied and wants – no more from me at present."

"That's the best news I've heard for a long time," Nanny said tartly. "I never did approve of you listenin' at keyholes as if you were one of the servants."

"Now we can enjoy ourselves," Ivana said, "and perhaps, although the Earl did not say so – the Marquis will be – leaving soon."

"And a good thing too!" Nanny said. "I'll be glad to see the back of him. I never did like them Froggies in peace or in war!"

"I am only afraid that if he goes, we shall have to go too," Ivana sighed.

"There's no need to cross that bridge till you comes to it," Nanny said, "and, if I knows his Lordship, if he has to turn us out of here, he'll find us somewhere else to live."

"Do you really think so?" Ivana enquired.

"I'm ever so sure of it," Nanny replied. "He's a gentleman born and bred and that's not somethin' I'd say about a lot of people."

Ivana realised that Nanny was referring to her stepfather and the dreadful Lord Hanford.

If she had indeed helped the Earl with his problems, she could only hope that somehow he would help her with hers.

'We cannot go on hiding for ever,' she thought desperately.

Then she told herself that perhaps the Earl could find some work for her to do out in the country.

There she could stay in a little cottage somewhere where her stepfather would never be able to find her.

'I must talk to the Earl about it the next time I see him,' she determined.

And then she paused and wondered how soon that would be.

*

The Marquis finished his breakfast.

Having waited on him, Smith came to find Ivana in the drawing room.

"Excuse me, miss," he began, "but Monsieur says he'll be in for luncheon and asks if you'll

~130~

honour him by bein' his guest. He'd also like to take you drivin' this afternoon in a phaeton."

Ivana was well aware that there was room only for two in a phaeton.

She knew it would be a mistake, after what the Earl had said about being pleasant to the Marquis, to refuse his invitation to luncheon.

But she recognised that she must not go alone with him in a phaeton.

"Will you tell Monsieur," she said slowly, "that Mrs. Bell and I would be delighted to have luncheon with him, but unfortunately we have an appointment for later in the afternoon that we cannot cancel."

"I'll tell him, miss," Smith replied, "but I suspects he'll be disappointed."

He did not wait for Ivana to say anything more but went into the study.

A few minutes later he came back.

"Monsieur, as I told you, miss, is very disappointed you can't go drivin' with him, but he's havin' a dinner party this evenin' and hopes you'll honour him by meetin' his friends."

There was nothing that Ivana could do but accept the invitation and she knew that Nanny would make some excuse not to be present.

The Marquis was very effusive at luncheon, talking about the parties that he had been invited to attend.

He said that it had been delightful to meet the exiled Royal Family of France, who were now resident in England.

He talked glibly of the Comtes de Lisle and d'Artois, the Ducs de Berri and de Bourbon.

Ivana was considerably impressed, especially when he talked about Louis XVI's only surviving child, the Duchesse d'Angoulême.

"And are you returning to France soon?" Nanny asked when he had repeated several times how delighted they had been to see him.

The Marquis was quiet for a moment before he said,

"I hope we shall all return when Napoleon Bonaparte is defeated."

"And the sooner the better in my opinion!" Nanny chimed in rather aggressively.

"That is, of course, what I think myself," the Marquis said, "but it does not appear that victory is yet in sight."

He spoke almost sadly, but watching him, Ivana thought that there was a sudden sparkle in his eyes that was somehow at variance with his words.

She had been sure when the Marquis talked of the French aristocrats in England that the Earl was wrong and that there was nothing suspicious about him.

Then some instinct of hers that she could not completely control told Ivana that the way he spoke was far too glib. And he did not in actual fact envisage Napoleon being defeated with Wellington's Army victorious.

'I may be wrong,' she thought to herself, 'but I cannot help how I feel.'

It was the same feeling she had had about him when he first arrived. He had established himself in London and had been accepted by quite a number of distinguished people.

Their invitations could all be seen displayed proudly on the mantelpiece in the study, but even so she was still suspicious.

Now he said, as if he wanted to convince her and Nanny even more than they were at the moment,

"I expect you have guessed where I am going tomorrow evening?"

"No, indeed, where?" Ivana asked.

"To a party that is being given by His Royal Highness the Prince Regent," the Marquis smiled in a self-satisfied manner.

"The Prince Regent is giving a party?" Ivana asked.

"It will be, I am quite certain, as delightful and impressive as those he has given before," the Marquis replied. "I told Viscount Palmerston when I arrived in London that I would like more than anything else to see the beauty and luxuriousness of Carlton House and, of course, attend one of His Royal Highness's renowned parties."

"Then you are very lucky," Ivana said. "I have read about them in the newspapers and they sound fascinating."

"That is what I am sure it will be and I will tell you all about it on Friday morning."

"I shall much look forward to that," Ivana remarked. "And please remember everything for me including the wonderful treasures that he has collected in Carlton House."

"I will do exactly as you tell me," the Marquis replied. "In fact, lovely Lady, to hear is to obey!"

He looked at Ivana in a way that made her feel embarrassed and Nanny said sharply,

"If you've now finished your luncheon, *monsieur*, I think Miss Ashley and I should be gettin' ready to go to our next appointment."

"You are going out?" the Marquis enquired.

"Yes, we are!" Nanny retorted firmly.

"Then I must reluctantly let you leave me," the Marquis said, "but only for the moment. You must not forget, Miss Ashley, that you have promised to dine with me and my friends at seven-thirty this evening."

"I am looking forward to it," Ivana replied, "but, of course, Smith will have told you that Mrs. Bell feels that she must refuse as late nights invariably make her feel ill the next day."

"I understand," the Marquis said. "But what is important is that my friends shall meet the charming and delightful hostess who has made me so welcome and happy in her attractive London home."

He bent a little nearer to Ivana as he added,

"In fact it is difficult to express in words how grateful l am to you, so I shall say it in a different way."

Before she realised what he was doing, he reached out, took her hand in his and kissed it.

His lips felt hot and greedy against the softness of her skin and she then felt an intense revulsion.

It was with difficulty that she did not snatch away her hand from him and tell him rudely not to touch her.

It felt almost as if she had come in contact with a serpent.

It was only with the greatest effort at self-control that she managed to smile.

She then drew away her hand without it appearing to be a rude movement.

Nanny had already risen to her feet and, as Ivana rose too, the Marquis said in a voice which only she could hear,

"Must you leave me? I do want to talk to you."

"We must not be late for our appointment," Ivana said quickly. "Thank you, *monsieur*, for asking us to have luncheon with you."

"You know without my saying so," he replied in a low voice, "that the pleasure, which is an inexpressible delight, is mine!"

Again he was looking at her in a way which made her feel frightened and a little unsure of herself.

Hastily, because Nanny was already standing at the door, she joined her.

As if she could not help herself, she looked back.

The Marquis was still seated at the table.

He was looking up at her and there was an expression on his face that made her feel that, like Lord Hanford, he desired her.

The thought was menacing.

CHAPTER SIX

Ivana and Nanny were in the drawing room before dinner when the Marquis came in.

Ivana felt a little guilty, as she had not seen him since the previous day and had not gone to the dinner that she had been invited to.

At the last moment she had thought that it would be a mistake for her to attend.

She had sent a message through Smith to explain that both she and Mrs. Bell had eaten something that had disagreed with them at luncheontime and they were therefore unable to accept his kind invitation.

Now, as he advanced down the room, she realised that he was dressed for going to the Prince Regent's party.

He was wearing evening clothes and there were a number of decorations which glittered in the light streaming in through the window from the setting sun.

"I came to say 'goodnight', *mademoiselle*," the Marquis said as he reached Ivana, "and I hope you are feeling better after your indisposition."

"I am much better, thank you, *monsieur*," Ivana replied, "and so very sorry to miss your dinner party."

"It is I who am sorry."

Because of the innuendo in his voice, Ivana responded quickly,

"I hope you enjoy yourself tonight. Permit me to say you are looking very smart."

"*Merci, mademoiselle*," the Marquis replied and then went on, "If you were coming with me, you would undoubtedly be the most beautiful lady present."

Ivana was just about to say that was very unlikely, when she realised that he had spoken in French.

By a split second she prevented herself from showing that she had understood what he had said.

With a supreme effort of will, she managed to reply,

"I-I am afraid — I don't understand what you say."

There was an expression in the Marquis's eyes that she did not like.

He had set a trap for her.

Although she had not fallen into it, she thought that he was not convinced that she was as ignorant of the French language as she appeared to be.

"I must go now," he said, speaking in English, "and tomorrow I will tell you all about the party and how fabulous it undoubtedly was."

"I shall look forward to that," Ivana said, "and remember to look at the many treasures which His Royal Highness has collected. I have read about them in the newspapers."

"I most certainly will," the Marquis agreed, "because you have asked me to do so."

He walked towards the door and when he reached it he looked back.

There was not only an expression in his eyes that reminded her of Lord Hanford but also, she thought, one of suspicion.

She waited until he had crossed the hall and then heard him saying 'goodnight', to Smith, who was holding open the door, before she allowed her agitation at nearly having made a serious mistake to show.

She turned to Nanny and confessed,

"I very nearly answered him in French and then he would have known that I was a spy!"

"The sooner you stop all this nonsense the better," Nanny commented archly.

Ivana was silent for a few moments.

Then she said,

"The Earl will be wearing the decorations that he has won in the War. It seems strange, Nanny, that if the Marquis has been incarcerated in prison for so long, he still has his! Surely, his French captors would have taken them from him or he would have forced to sell them."

"I'd expect he thought up some hanky-panky to keep them safe," Nanny replied, "but I do agree with you, dearie, it does seem ever so strange, seeing as we heard how terrible bad them prisoners in France was bein' treated."

Ivana sighed.

Her heart ached for the ten thousand tourists who had been interned by the French back in 1804 when hostilities were renewed against England after a brief truce.

Napoleon Bonaparte's action of interning them, because the British had sunk one of his ships, was unprecedented in the history of war.

Everyone in England and the free countries had declared it an act against humanity.

The prisoners, however, could not escape and for all of eight years they had languished on hostile soil with no chance of coming back to their own people and living in deplorable conditions.

Was it possible that the Marquis, who declared himself an enemy of the new *Régime*, would *not* have been robbed of what were obviously his most precious possessions?

She thought that it was something that she should ask the Earl about the next time that she saw him.

Sitting down at the table where Nanny was sewing, she started to help her, while all the time continuing to think about the Marquis.

*

Driving towards Carlton House, the Earl realised that although it was still very early, St. James's Street and the Haymarket were full of carriages.

Because his coachman was almost as skilful as his Master, they managed to pass most of them with considerable ease.

They therefore arrived at Carlton House without having to wait for too long in a queue.

A large Band of the Grenadier Guards was playing in the courtyard beneath the fine Corinthian portico, which had been designed by Henry Holland.

When the Earl stepped out of his carriage, he was received warmly in the hall of fine Ionic columns by members of the Regent's household.

They were all delighted to see the Earl and looked upon him as a hero, having heard the praise that had been heaped on him by the Duke of Wellington himself.

The Earl wandered through several magnificent rooms until he found the Prince Regent waiting to greet his guests.

He was wearing the richly embroidered uniform of a Field Marshal. It was a rank that he had aspired to for a long time before he finally attained it.

His father, King George III, had steadfastly barred him from the appointment and for no particular reason.

Tonight he was wearing the glittering Star of the Most Noble Order of the Garter and a splendid egret.

He was now forty-nine years old, but he looked, the Earl thought, somewhat older. He was still very handsome, but undoubtedly much too fat, although he had lost a little weight lately.

At one time he had turned the scales at over seventeen and a half stone.

But he still had the charm and exquisite manners that had won him the nickname of 'The First Gentleman of Europe'.

He was also, as the Earl knew, exceedingly amusing and had a wit that was outstanding, even among a number of his friends, who were noted for the brilliance of their conversation.

Having been greeted effusively by the Prince Regent, the Earl moved out into the garden.

Like all of the Prince's parties or rather fêtes, they were designed in the most lavish and extravagant manner.

Special buildings had been erected for dinner and flowers, both fresh and artificial, were laid out so that the garden appeared to be a bower of soft beauty.

There was a covered promenade, the interior decorated with draperies and rose-coloured cords, which then led to a Corinthian Temple where all the walls were decorated with green calico.

In other parts of the garden there were supper tents and refreshment rooms with rose-coloured curtains and the flowers attached to them were scenting the air.

The Earl was aware that this was one of the smaller parties that the Prince Regent had arranged.

He reckoned, however, that there would be at least a five hundred people there before the party ended. As these were most of the Prince Regent's personal friends, the women were not only beautiful but spectacular wearing a profusion of glorious and valuable jewels.

Each one was trying their best to out-rival the other with a gown that came from the most expensive dressmakers found on Bond Street.

In the main supper room there was a miniature fountain on the most important table, over which the host would preside, where water flowed constantly into a silver-bedded stream that was bounded by mossy banks, water plants and flowers.

The Earl, however, gave all this splendour only a perfunctory glance before he moved across the garden to where there was a high wall separating the gardens from The Mall.

The Prince Regent had planted the most exquisite shrubs and trees in front of the wall and they were all now in blossom.

The Earl was aware that these bushes concealed a number of people who were essential to the plan he had drawn up, which was to take place later in the evening.

He glanced round and then moved back into the house.

More and more people were arriving and a great number of his personal friends greeted him excitedly.

"You are much better, my Lord," one beautiful woman cooed at him, "and now you have no excuse not to visit me, as I so wish you to do."

She looked up at him with an invitation in her eyes and a provocative pout to her lips.

"I will certainly do so as soon as it is possible," the Earl replied.

"If it is possible for you to come here tonight, then it is possible for you to come to me!" the beautiful lady continued in a low voice.

He smiled at her, but then tactfully made her no promises.

As he excused himself and moved away from her, she looked after him with an irritated expression on her face. She knew all too well that he was being elusive, as so many other women had complained that he was in the past.

Every room in the house was filling up with those who wanted either to see or be seen.

Among them were a number of people who knew that, every time they came to Carlton House, there would be more treasures on display to admire and talk about.

There would be more pictures, statues and furniture, which the Prince Regent acquired day by day for his various collections.

At exactly nine o'clock the Prince Regent led the way rather pompously in for dinner.

There was a scramble to sit at his table, but it was inevitable that many guests would be disappointed.

They could not complain in any way, however, about the delicious food that was served by the Prince's servants. They were wearing dark blue livery trimmed with gold lace.

There were hot soups, roast meats of every sort to choose from and plenty of cold dishes, all exquisitely cooked by the Prince Regent's own team of chefs.

There were endless grapes, peaches, pineapple and every other sort of fruit in profusion, together with iced champagne and other wines.

The Earl thought that only the Prince Regent could make everything run so smoothly so that nobody felt neglected and no one had to wait.

He was being at his most charming and amusing and everyone around him was laughing.

Only as the long-drawn-out menu of copious courses came to an end did the Earl move away from the main table.

He was looking for the Marquis and then saw him surrounded by French *émigrés* who were obviously making a great fuss over him.

He did not approach them. Instead he watched from a distance while also talking to some friends who had hurried up to have a quiet word with him.

He knew that they were all very eager to talk about the War and to find out what was happening in France.

When the Prince Regent was about to leave his table, the Earl noticed that the Marquis was moving.

Appearing as if he was not going to do so, he then sneaked down towards the wall that divided the garden from The Mall.

There were a number of things to look at on the way, small fountains illuminated so that water thrown up into the air seemed to fall like a thousand rainbows, beautiful sculptures and lovely flowers.

Only the Earl had noticed that the Marquis had suddenly disappeared into the bushes that bordered the lawns.

When he emerged only a few minutes later, the Earl at once saw that he had unbolted the garden gate.

It was used so seldom that the Prince Regent had not thought it necessary to have it guarded, as were the gates that led from the front of the house into The Mall.

There was, as the Earl knew, no lock, only two strong bolts to prevent anyone from entering from the outside.

The Marquis was now moving nonchalantly back into the nearest crowd of people and started talking animatedly to them.

Nevertheless the Earl's eagle eye was aware of more movements in the bushes along the outside wall and moving nearer to the garden gate.

It was then he walked quickly back towards the house and, finding the Prince Regent just having left the supper room, he said to him,

"If Your Royal Highness is not too busy, would you be extremely gracious and show me the new picture by Poussin that I hear you have recently purchased?"

The Prince Regent's eyes lit up.

"You have heard about it then?"

"I have heard, sir, and I long to see it," the Earl replied, "but, of course, if Your Royal Highness is too busy – "

"I am never too busy to talk to you, Lorimer," the Prince Regent said as he smiled. "Of course, come and see my picture and personally I think it is a great find, but then you may not agree."

"I have never known you to be wrong when it comes to a picture or a statue, Sire," the Earl answered.

The Prince Regent was clearly delighted at this remark.

He started to tell the Earl how he had seen the picture so dark with grime that those who were with him told him that he must be crazy to think it was even worth having cleaned.

"I insisted," the Prince Regent stated, "and, when the dirt was cleaned away, there were exquisite colours underneath that Poussin had painted. Quite, quite lovely!"

"It was very clever of you, Sire," the Earl enthused.

The Price Regent guided him to the music room where the picture now hung.

He continued to tell more of the story of the picture and of how he had found it.

The Earl appeared to be listening attentively, but his mind was on what was happening in the garden.

*

As soon as he and the Prince Regent had disappeared inside the house, a figure emerged from behind the bushes and had walked slowly to the first fountain.

He appeared to be a large man and he was wearing the uniform of a Field Marshal.

As he stared up at the falling water from the fountain, he had his back to the garden door.

It opened slowly and, as the Earl had anticipated, Pier slipped inside.

It was impossible to guess what weapon he would use to try to kill the Prince Regent.

While Viscount Palmerston was expecting it to be a gun of some sort, the Earl was more convinced that he would use a dagger.

The Officer who now impersonated the Prince Regent was a slim man, but was padded out and wearing exactly the same clothes as the Prince Regent would do at a formal party.

It would be impossible, seeing him from behind, for Pier not to think that his prey was more easily accessible than he had expected.

Pier was dressed in exactly the same way as the Marquis in evening clothes.

If he circulated amongst the guests, it was doubtful that anybody would be suspicious of him.

Now, as he moved up behind the man in the Field Marshal's uniform, he drew from the inside of his cutaway coat a long slim dagger, very similar to a stiletto.

It could pierce any man's heart and be completely lethal at one stroke.

Pier raised his arm and the sharp point of the dagger cut through the heavily padded coat of the Field Marshal.

It could not, however, penetrate the armoured vest that was worn beneath it.

The victim staggered, but he did not fall.

Before he could draw back his dagger and strike again, Pier was seized on both sides by two resolute Officers of the Grenadier Guards.

They moved him so swiftly to the garden door that no one noticed what had transpired, not even those who were only a short distance away.

The Officer wearing the Field Marshal's uniform also disappeared into the bushes.

Two other Officers, however, came in through the garden gate and then walked across the lawn.

The Earl, who had just left the Prince Regent talking to some guests, saw them and he looked at them enquiringly.

The Officer nearest to him, who was a Major, just nodded his head slightly.

The Earl sighed deeply with relief.

He watched as the two Officers walked towards the Marquis. He was just emerging from the tent where he had dined with a number of his countrymen.

The two Officers walked up to him.

When they closed in on either side of him, he knew without asking any questions that his plan to murder the Prince Regent had failed abysmally.

He said nothing as he walked back between them to the door that he had opened earlier.

Only as he did so, did he draw something from the inner pocket of his coat.

He put it into his mouth.

Just as they reached the bushes that covered the garden door, he collapsed.

Watching, the Earl knew that even as the Officers' arms went out to try and support him, the Marquis was dead.

He turned immediately and walked back into the house.

He avoided the chattering groups of people who were then admiring the Prince Regent's possessions.

He was just about to find his way to the hall, when a servant came hurrying towards him.

"I've been lookin' for your Lordship," he said breathlessly. "There be a woman below as wants to speak to your Lordship immediate. Says 'tis a matter of life and death!"

The Earl did not ask him any questions, he merely hurried into the hall where he found Nanny.

She was looking very agitated and when she saw him she exclaimed,

"Oh, my Lord! My Lord, he's taken my baby and there were nothin' I could do about it!"

She was obviously extremely upset, but at the same time she was wise enough to keep her voice low.

"Who has taken Miss Ivana?" the Earl asked quickly.

"Lord Hanford, 'twas him as she was a-hidin' from."

"But, why?" the Earl enquired.

"Because her stepfather, my Lord, an evil man if ever there was one, had sold Miss Ivana to Lord Hanford for five-thousand pounds! Five-thousand pounds, my Lord! 'Twas wicked, that's what 'twas!"

"I agree with you," the Earl nodded.

He turned to the nearest servant.

"Call for my carriage at once," he ordered sharply.

"Very good, my Lord."

The servant went out through the front door.

"Now, listen, Nanny," the Earl said, "have you any idea where Lord Hanford has taken Miss Ivana?"

"'Twas terrible, my Lord, terrible!" Nanny said. "He comes in, seizes her by the arm afore she could escape. Then his servants tied a rope round her body and her feet together! While they were a-doin' that, his Lordship put a gag over her mouth, a gag, my Lord. Oh, that wicked, wicked man!"

"Did he say anything? Did he mention where he was taking her?" the Earl persisted.

"They trusses her up like a chicken, they did," Nanny went on. "He puts a cape over her shoulders and says, 'I am takin' you home and you'll not escape me again'!"

Nanny gave a little sob before she added,

"They carries her off, my Lord, and pushes her into the carriage and drives off. There were nothin' I could do – nothin' except come here and tell you all about it."

"That was very sensible of you, Nanny," the Earl praised her.

"Do you think they'll take her to his Lordship's house in the country?" Nanny asked.

"If so, I know where it is," the Earl answered.

As he spoke, a servant came to his side with his cape and helped him into it.

The Earl took his hat from him and said,

"One thing more, Nanny, what vehicle was he travelling in?"

"'Twas one of them new-fangled travellin' bratchkas," Nanny said, "and that evil man were a-drivin' it himself."

"With two horses, I suppose?"

"Two horses," Nanny confirmed.

The Earl patted Nanny on the arm.

"Go home, Nanny, and don't worry about anything. I will rescue her."

"God bless your Lordship," Nanny said, "I knows that was what you'd do and God help you."

"I will need His help," the Earl replied, "so do keep on praying."

He turned as he spoke and went out through the door and into the courtyard.

As he was one of the first guests to arrive, his carriage was there waiting for him.

Viscount Palmerston was determined, once his plan to catch the assailant had succeeded, that he should not in any way become embroiled.

The Earl had therefore arranged to leave the party early and drive straight to his house in the country.

He had his new four-in-hand carriage, which he had designed himself, waiting for him.

He had intended to rest his injured leg and sleep all the way as his coachman drove it to Lorimer Park.

As he then walked outside, he climbed up into the driver's seat, saying to his coachman's surprise,

"I will drive and Jim can climb up behind."

The carriage was very light, it had a seat at the front for a coachman and footman and there was another seat behind if it was required.

The Earl knew that his horses were fresh and ready to go and so could overtake anything that Lord Hanford was driving.

At the same time he was not certain how great a start Hanford had.

As he drove out of the courtyard at Carlton House and into The Mall, he knew that this was going to be the greatest challenge he had ever faced in his life.

If he was to rescue Ivana, it would require both his brain and all his expertise.

And he well knew that to leave her with Lord Hanford would be a terrifying experience for her that would scar her for life.

It was one that she would find it hard to ever forget.

'God help her until I reach her!' the Earl asserted under his breath.

It was the sincerest prayer he had uttered since he was a small boy.

*

Half-lying and half-sitting beside Lord Hanford in the travelling bratchka, Ivana could hardly believe what had happened to her.

Nanny had just put away her sewing and suggested that it was time for them to go to bed.

"I'm findin' all this sewin' ever so tirin' on me eyes, dearie," she moaned.

"Then you must not do it, Nanny dearest," Ivana scolded her. "You don't want to wear spectacles. They are very unbecoming."

Nanny had laughed.

"That does not matter to me at my age! At the same time none of us wants to be blind."

"That is true enough," Ivana agreed.

"Well, well go to bed," Nanny said, "and don't you lie awake, wishin' you were still at Carlton

House dancin' round with all them fancy overdressed people!"

Ivana laughed.

"Of course, I wish I was there. Think how beautiful everything must look, Nanny. They say that His Royal Highness has fountains in the gardens. It is massed with flowers and the food is amazing and delicious."

"It sounds all right," Nanny agreed, "but it's not for the likes of us. If you asks me, that Frenchman's got no right to be there, guzzlin' and drinkin' while his kith and kin are killin' our men."

"The Marquis was certainly very pleased to be invited as a guest," Ivana remarked.

She was wondering as she spoke if he really was a spy for the French.

In any case, even if he was, it was hardly likely he could do anything at the party while the Earl was there with a great number of other Officers.

As well, of course, countless sentries and an army of servants.

She had read in one of the newspapers of the enormous crowd of Equerries and servants employed at Carlton House.

And there was His Royal Highness's Treasurer, his Private Secretary, Assistant Private Secretary, his Vice-Treasurer and his Vice-Chancellor.

Then there was the Keeper of the Wardrobe and a Gentleman Porter as well as those 'below stairs'. As well there two clerks, five Pages of the Presence, five Pages of the Back Stairs and a housekeeper.

There was an Inspector of the Household, a *Maitre d'Hôtel*, a butler, a Table Decker, two surgeons and forty-three other servants.

Included with these there was a silver scullery-woman, a laundress, two cellarmen, three compressionists, four watchmen, six cooks and fifteen housemaids.

Ivana had laughed at the time to think that it could be possible that one man should want so many staff to care for his every whim and make his life ever more comfortable.

She was sure, however, that, if nothing else, they would look after the Prince Regent and protect him from England's sworn enemies.

They should certainly be able to guard him from any plotting that the French might make against his life.

Of course the Earl would be there too to prevent His Royal Highness from being hurt in any way.

'He is wonderful!' she pondered to herself, thinking of the Earl.

She and Nanny walked into the hall.

As they did so, Smith came hurrying out of the kitchen.

"I've just heard, miss," he said to Ivana, "there's been a victory in France. Someone as come to the kitchen door was tellin' me and the missus about it. It sounds as if things be a-movin' out there at last!"

"That is very good news!" Ivana exclaimed.

"I thought I'd just pop out then," Smith continued, "and see if I can get a newspaper in Parliament Square."

"I think that is a good idea," Ivana agreed.

"I thought you'd want to know, miss. I'll go and fetch the key."

"Don't worry about that," Ivana said, "I will open the door to you."

"All right, miss, and I won't be long," Smith replied.

He opened the front door, let himself out and closed it again behind him.

"A victory, Nanny!" Ivana cried excitedly. "That means the War will soon be over!"

"I hope so," Nanny answered, "there's been enough killin' and sufferin' because of that dreadful man Napoleon. I wants to hear no more of it."

"And so do I," Ivana said in a low voice.

She was thinking of her father and also that the Earl was lucky to have only a wound in his leg.

He too, like the man who had owned this house, might have been killed.

Nanny went slowly up the stairs.

"I'm goin' to my room," she told Ivana, "and, when Smith brings back the newspaper, come and tell me what's happened."

"Of course I will," Ivana replied. "I don't suppose he will be very long."

It was about two minutes later and Nanny had just reached the landing, when there was a knock on the door.

Ivana ran to it and flung it open.

"You have been very qui – !" she started to say.

Then she stopped.

Standing outside was not Smith but *Lord Hanford*.

Because she was so astonished to see him, Ivana could only stand and stare at him.

Then, as he moved nearer, she started to back away from him.

"So here you are!" he almost shouted in his thick voice. "And a fine dance you have led me!"

"Wh-what do – you – want?" Ivana asked in a whisper.

"I want you!" Lord Hanford replied threateningly.

She would have turned to run away from him, but he reached out and caught hold of her arm.

As he did so, two of his servants came running into the hall.

Almost before Ivana could realise what was happening, they had wound a rope around her body, binding her arms to her sides.

Another of Lord Hanford's servants then tied her ankles together with the same rope.

"What — are you — doing? How — dare you — touch me!" she tried to shout out, but it was only a whimper.

It was then that Lord Hanford pulled a gag over her mouth and tied it tightly behind her head.

"That will stop you from screaming for assistance!" he said. "Nor will you be able to run away from me."

One of the servants who had tied her legs brought a fur-lined cape, which he put over her shoulders.

Lord Hanford then pulled the hood of it over her head so that it hid part of her face.

"Now I am taking you home," he gloated, "and you will never run away from me again."

It was a threat rather than a statement.

As Nanny watched helplessly at the top of the stairs, she realised that it would be quite impossible for her to intervene.

She saw Ivana being lifted up by the servants and they then carried her out to the carriage that was waiting outside the front door.

Nanny heard it driving away.

She knew at once that somehow she had to reach the Earl as quickly as possible and tell him about Lord Hanford and what had happened to Ivana.

CHAPTER SEVEN

It had all happened so fast.

Ivana could hardly believe that she was not dreaming and would soon wake up and find herself still in her comfortable bed.

As Lord Hanford drove on, she was aware that the travelling bratchka had no doors but was open at the sides.

There was just the front against which the driver rested his feet.

The rope that had been tied so tightly round her ankles was causing her pain, as was the gag in her mouth.

She was just as conscious that the wind had blown a little of her hair over her eyes.

Although she tried her best to flick it away, it remained there, tickling and irritating her so that she wanted to scream out.

She was well aware that the reason Lord Hanford had gagged her so tightly was so that she could not cry for help.

He had ensured most successfully that she could not get away from his clutches in any way.

He was driving very fast, she thought, and rather dangerously.

She suspected that he had been drinking heavily before he came to the house.

Having negotiated a certain amount of traffic, he said in a thick voice,

"I expect you are wondering, Ivana, how I found you. I am a good deal cleverer than you imagined I would be."

As Ivana could not answer him, he carried on,

"Your stepfather, as you might well guess, was distraught and quite useless, but I kept my head and used my brain."

He was obviously very pleased with himself, Ivana reckoned, and after a short pause he went on,

"I realised how much you had taken away from the house, which, according to your stepfather, was everything that had any value in that pokey hole. I knew that you must have hired a conveyance of some sort."

He chuckled and it was an unpleasant sound before he continued,

"When I questioned a good number of the drivers of Hackney carriages, they all claimed that they had no knowledge at all of any pretty girl and an elderly woman with a mountain of belongings."

Ivana was beginning to realise what had happened and Lord Hanford confirmed it when he finished,

"The man who took you from Islington to Queen Anne Street actually turned up late this afternoon. His horse had been ill, doubtless due to the weight you had put on him."

'So that is how he knew where I was,' Ivana thought despairingly.

"And so I found you and caught you!" Lord Hanford was saying with a note of triumph in his voice. "And you will not get away from me another time, my girl, I will make very sure of that!"

They were now travelling over a road lit by bright moonlight.

Lord Hanford reached down under his seat with his right hand and brought out a flask.

He opened it with some difficulty and then drank for several seconds.

Then he said in an even thicker voice than he had spoken in before,

"It's a pity you cannot join me, but I will give you something to cheer you up after I have punished you for making me so worried as to where you had disappeared to."

His words made Ivana shiver.

She knew only too well what he meant.

She now remembered how he had told her stepfather that he whipped his horses and his women into doing what he wanted.

'I must – die,' she thought despairingly, 'die before he – touches me.'

She was wondering if there was a lake near Lord Hanford's country house. She could not swim and she remembered reading somewhere that death by drowning was supposedly not too unpleasant.

Even if it was terrifying, it could not be worse than being in the clutches of an evil and violent man.

There was no doubt that the brandy, or whatever was in the flask, did not improve his driving. A little farther on they missed, just by inches, a cart filled with vegetables.

Ivana thought that his driving was indeed another way that she might easily die before she reached Lord Hanford's house.

If she did not, what would she do?

What *could* she do?

It was then that she began to pray that God, if He would not save her, would show her the least painful way to kill herself.

Then, like a bright light in the darkness, she knew that Nanny would somehow be able to get in touch with the Earl.

She knew where he was, but at the same time she would have to find a Hackney carriage to carry her to Carlton House.

Perhaps when she arrived there the servants would not let her in to tell the Earl what had happened.

Ivana then remembered with horror that he had said he might not be able to see her for two or three days. That meant, she thought, that he was going away somewhere after he had dined with the Prince Regent at Carlton House.

'Please God – let Nanny find him – before he goes away – please – *please* – '

She was praying so very intensely that for the moment she had forgotten the tightness of the gag or that her feet were becoming numb.

'Please – God – *please* – '

She looked up at the stars and wondered if they would carry her message up to Heaven.

'Help me – *help me*!'

It was then that she knew that she was praying to the Earl.

She not only wanted to see him so he would save her but also because she loved him and could not imagine never seeing him again.

*

The Earl settled down to drive his team of thoroughbreds with the expertise that he was famous for. It made his coachman watch him in growing admiration.

The Earl was thinking what a blessing it was that he had his four-in-hand available for him in London.

If it was humanly possible, he would be able to overtake Lord Hanford on the road.

Equally there was some anxiety in his eyes as he knew that there was just a chance that Lord Hanford would not be actually taking Ivana to his country house in Hertfordshire, but somewhere else.

He was a rich man and he might easily have a house at Newmarket or Leicestershire for the racing and hunting.

The road ahead was empty.

The well-matched team of horses that the Earl was driving had rested well for it had been two days since they had come up from the country.

There was no need for the lamps to be lit on either side of the carriage, the road was as clear as daylight.

As there had been no rain, the surface of the road was firm if rather dusty.

On and on the Earl went, but there was no sign of any other vehicle ahead of him.

At this stage Lord Hanford's house was only about three or four miles farther on down the road.

The Earl knew it well because his own house was little more than ten miles away.

But, although they lived in the same County, his father would never have condescended to know Lord Hanford. He himself, having served in the War, had never come into contact with him.

He was, nevertheless, aware of his reputation and that he was a coarse unpleasant fellow who was cruel to his horses.

The idea of Ivana being in his power made the Earl set his lips in a determined tight line.

Almost by sheer willpower he increased the speed of his team and they covered a long stretch of straight road in record time.

It was then the Earl saw at the end of it the raised hood of what he knew was a travelling bratchka.

He felt his heart leap in his chest.

He had won.

He would now be able to save Ivana.

*

Ivana was in despair.

After Lord Hanford drank the last drop of what was in his flask, he slurred,

"Only a few more miles – my pretty one, then I will take your ropes from you and a great many other things you are wearing as well!"

He chuckled evilly after he had spoken.

Once again Ivana was praying that she might die.

It was then, as the road widened a little, that she was aware of the sound of horses' hoofs and wheels.

She knew at once that they did not belong to the carriage that she was travelling in.

By a superb piece of driving the Earl passed the bratchka at speed with barely an inch to spare on either side.

Going a little way further down the road, he pulled his team across it.

There was nothing that Lord Hanford could do but draw in his horses.

They came to a standstill only a few yards from the Earl's carriage.

Without hurrying the Earl handed his reins to his coachman and stepped down from the box.

Then he walked round his carriage and, with his tall hat set at an angle on his dark hair, he walked towards Lord Hanford.

Lord Hanford, crimson in the face with fury, watched him until he was within earshot.

Then he thundered,

"What the devil do you think you are doing, Lorimer, holding me up like this?"

The Earl came nearer still.

In a slow drawl that was insulting in itself, he replied,

"You are apparently unaware, I assume, Hanford, that the penalty for abducting a minor is transportation."

"I know the Law as well as you do," Lord Hanford retorted furiously, "and, as I have her Guardian's permission, Ivana is mine!"

For a moment there was silence.

Listening, Ivana felt despair. Perhaps the Earl would accept what Lord Hanford had said and go away.

She wanted to plead with him to stay and to tell him that, if he left her, she would die.

And she loved him – yes – she loved him with all her heart.

It seemed to her as if a century passed before the Earl replied in a quiet dignified voice,

"I suppose I must excuse your appalling behaviour, Hanford, because you are obviously unaware that Ivana is my wife."

Lord Hanford's jaw dropped.

Then he spluttered,

"Your wife? I don't believe it! When were you married?"

"Unfortunately," the Earl replied, "I do not have the marriage certificate with me, but if you call at my house tomorrow, one of my servants will show it to you."

He walked nearer to the carriage and looked down at Ivana.

"Now," he said, "I will take my wife home with me and if you ever touch or insult her again, I will call you out."

He bent forward as he spoke and picked Ivana up in his arms.

There was nothing that Lord Hanford could do.

He was well aware that the Earl was a noted shot and he had, before he had gone to the War, fought two duels in which he had easily been the victor.

Grinding his teeth, he watched as the Earl walked away with Ivana in his arms.

He lifted her gently onto the back seat of his carriage and said to the footman who was holding open the door,

"Give me a knife and tell Abby to hold the horses in this position until I am ready."

He cut the ropes that bound Ivana's ankles and the rope round her body.

Having done so, he flung the pieces onto the road so that Lord Hanford could see what he was doing.

Then he went round the carriage and, getting in from the other side, ordered as he did so,

"Now take us home, Abby, as smoothly as possible."

The footman closed the door behind him and jumped up onto the box.

With gentle fingers the Earl pulled back the hood from Ivana's head and then untied the gag.

As her mouth was freed, she tried to speak, but found it quite impossible to even utter one word.

Instead she burst into floods of tears.

She hid her face against the Earl's shoulder and cried tempestuously as a child might have done.

The relief after what she had suffered swept away her self-control.

She cried and cried until she realised that he was gently stroking her hair.

"It's all right," he was saying quietly. "It is all over and this will never happen again."

"I-I thought you – would not – be able to f-find me and – and I would – have to d-die," Ivana sobbed and her voice was almost incoherent.

"But I *have* found you," the Earl smiled at her. "You are not going to die, my darling, but be very happy."

Ivana was suddenly still.

Had he really called her 'my darling' or had she imagined it?

She then raised her head to look at him.

He could see the tears on her cheeks, while her eyes were wide and frightened.

"You are quite, quite safe," he was now saying.

Then he kissed her.

Ivana felt as if the skies had opened and the stars had all fallen down and were twinkling in her heart and shining in her eyes.

She knew as the Earl kissed her and went on kissing her that she had reached Heaven.

'I love – you! *I – love – you!*' she wanted to say, but it was just impossible to speak only to feel.

It must have been a long time later when she realised that the horses were slowing down.

They were passing down an oak tree bordered drive.

The Earl raised his head.

"We are home, my precious," he declared, "and now you can go to bed and get some sleep."

"I-I want to be – with you," Ivana whispered.

"That is what I want too," he answered, "but we are to be married first thing tomorrow morning."

"M-married? Do you – really mean – *married*?"

"I dislike telling lies," the Earl replied, "and in addition, I have no wish to encounter Lord Hanford again or indeed your stepfather."

"How can we – avoid it?" Ivana asked nervously.

"We are going to run away! I will tell you all about it tomorrow after we are married."

As he spoke, the carriage came to a standstill.

Ivana saw a red carpet being laid down over the steps up to the front door and footmen in colourful livery were waiting for them.

The Earl climbed out first.

Then, as he knew that Ivana would find it hard to walk, he went round to the other side and lifted her in his arms and he carried her up the steps to the front door where the butler was standing.

"We have an unexpected guest, Dawson," he said. "Tell Mrs. Meadows I want her."

"She's waiting, my Lord, upstairs, just in case your Lordship required anything. It's good to have your Lordship back with us."

"Thank you," the Earl smiled.

He walked up the stairs, holding Ivana tightly in his arms.

On the landing Mrs. Meadows, the housekeeper, was dressed in rustling black silk with a silver chatelaine at her waist. She dropped the Earl a deep curtsey.

"Good evening, my Lord, it's ever so good to see you again."

"And I am glad to see you, Mrs. Meadows," the Earl said. "This is Miss Ivana Sherard, who has been in an unfortunate accident and must go to bed at once and rest after her ordeal."

"Oh, the poor young lady!" Mrs. Meadows exclaimed. "Fortunately the bed in the room next to your Lordship's is made up and she'll be ever so comfortable there."

The Earl did not answer, he merely took Ivana along the corridor and into a magnificent room that had been his mother's.

He put her gently down on the bed, but she still clung to him.

"Will – you come and – see me later?" she asked. "And tell me – what is – happening?"

"I will," the Earl replied as he smiled.

He went from the room as Mrs. Meadows, still making consoling sounds, helped Ivana to undress.

It was over an hour later when the Earl, who had given orders that had put the whole household into a tumult, came upstairs.

At the top of the stairs he found that Mrs. Meadows was waiting for him.

"I've just put the young lady to bed, my Lord," she reported. "And I don't think there's anythin' more I can do to help her."

The Earl smiled.

"There is a great deal, Mrs. Meadows! Miss Sherard is marrying me first thing tomorrow morning and we are going away on our honeymoon."

"Oh, my Lord!" Mrs. Meadows exclaimed. "That be good news, very good news indeed! We've all been hopin' you'd take a wife and a prettier young lady I've never seen."

"That is what I think too," the Earl replied, "but she has nothing with her but what she stands up in, so I want you to find her enough clothes for us to take away on our honeymoon until I can send for some gowns from London."

Mrs. Meadows did not gasp or even expostulate.

She merely responded,

"There's plenty of your Lordship's grandmother's gowns, which I thinks'll be about the right size. There's also, my Lord, a number of other gowns that we've accumulated over the years."

"I will leave it to you, Mrs. Meadows," the Earl said. "My wife will also need a lady's maid who can alter anything that is required immediately."

"I'll see to it, my Lord," Mrs. Meadows promised.

"I knew you would. You have never failed me yet, not once."

Mrs. Meadows beamed.

"You're takin' just the sort of wife I'd have chosen for your Lordship if you'd asked me," she said, "and I'd swear on the Bible that you're goin' to be really happy."

The Earl then put his hand on Mrs. Meadows's shoulder before he walked off down the corridor.

As he entered Ivana's room, he saw that there was a candle burning beside the bed.

When he reached her, however, she was fast asleep.

Her fair hair was spread out over the pillows and her eyelashes, which turned up like a child's, were the only colour in her pale face.

He knew that she was thoroughly exhausted and worn out with the fear and terror that she had been subjected to when Lord Hanford had taken her away from the house in London.

He could understand only too well her feelings of disgust for such a man.

He stood very still for a long time, gazing down at her.

There was a sudden expression of tenderness in his eyes that no woman had ever seen.

Then he blew out the candle and went from the room, closing the door quietly behind him.

*

Ivana was woken by the maid pulling back the curtains.

As she opened her eyes, Mrs. Meadows came into the room with her breakfast on a tray.

"Good mornin', miss," she began. "When you're up and dressed, his Lordship wants you downstairs as soon as it be possible."

Ivana sat up in bed.

"I-I have slept – all night!" she said.

"That's just what was best for you," Mrs. Meadows exclaimed, "so hurry now, miss, and eat your breakfast. There's a great deal to do today."

Ivana laughed a little with sheer happiness.

She ate the delicious breakfast provided for her by the Earl's chef while the maids were bringing in her bath.

When she came out of the scented water, they helped her to dry.

Then she put on a pretty white gown, which Mrs. Meadows told her had belonged to the Earl's grandmother.

"'Tis a gown her Ladyship never wore," she informed Ivana. "She loved pretty things and, even when she was old, she had her gowns sent down from Bond Street. No one was brave enough to tell her that she'd never wear them. But I knows her Ladyship would be glad to see you in them."

The gown was more elaborate and certainly more expensive than anything that Ivana had ever owned.

It was white and trimmed with tiny rows of shadow lace, both round the puffed sleeves and the deep hem. Silver ribbons crossed under her breasts and tied into bows to fall down her back to the floor.

"It might have been made for me!" Ivana exclaimed.

"It needed to be taken in just a little at the waist," Mrs. Meadows confessed. "I had the seamstress up at five o'clock this mornin' and she's been workin' on a number of gowns that you'll be takin' with you, miss."

Ivana gave a cry of delight.

She did not ask questions, however, knowing that the Earl wanted to tell her where they were going.

Then there was a knock on the door and, when the maid opened it, she came back with a wreath of flowers.

"His Lordship's compliments, miss," she announced, "and he says as he wishes to leave immediate-like after the Weddin' so he'd like you to wear this wreath rather than a veil."

The wreath was really lovely and was made of small white roses, lilies-of-the-valley and just a few orchids.

When Ivana went downstairs, there was a bouquet of the same flowers waiting for her in the hall.

And so was the Earl.

He was looking exceedingly smart. His intricately tied cravat was very high and could rival anything worn by the Prince Regent. At the same time he was dressed in his travelling clothes and his Hessian boots shone like mirrors.

He watched Ivana coming down the stairs.

As she reached the bottom step, he took her hands in his and kissed them one after the other.

Then he gave her his arm.

Without speaking they then walked down a long corridor that led eventually to the Earl's Private Chapel.

The Earl's Private Chaplain was waiting for them in the Chapel and somebody unseen was playing softly on the organ.

The Marriage Service was very moving.

As Ivana knelt with the Earl for the Blessing, she realised that no one could be more blessed than she was.

At last she was safe and, as the Earl's wife, no one could ever hurt her again.

When they rose to their feet, the Earl gave her his arm. And then they walked out of the Chapel and back into the hall.

Mrs. Meadows bustled forward with a blue cape that had a white fur collar and was very becoming.

Ivana saw waiting outside on the drive that there was a phaeton drawn by a different team of horses from those that the Earl was driving the previous night.

Behind it there was a brake, in which she knew that her lady's maid would travel as well as the Earl's valet.

The footmen were currently piling a number of quite heavy trunks into the brake.

Ivana thought how fortunate it was that Mrs. Meadows had been able to find her so many pretty and stylish things to wear.

As they went down the steps on the red carpet, the footmen and a number of housemaids threw rose petals and rice at them.

They climbed into the phaeton and the Earl drove off, laughing as he exclaimed,

"That was something I did not order!"

"They wanted to wish us luck," Ivana reckoned.

"That is exactly what we have already," he replied.

She looked up and drew nearer to him.

"Now you must tell me where we are going," she wanted to know.

"I told you we are running away," the Earl answered, "and nobody will know where we are.

We will be alone and I can tell you, my darling, a great deal about love and my deep love for you."

Ivana pressed her cheek for a second against his shoulder.

"How could I know, how – could I – guess," she asked, "that when I – prayed for you to – save me that you also – loved me?"

"I have loved you for a long time," the Earl answered, "at least it seems so to me. But I thought, because we were both engaged in something of great importance to our country, that it must come first."

Ivana drew in her breath.

"I had forgotten – it is terrible of me to – have forgotten – but was everything – all right– I mean about the Marquis?"

"He is dead," the Earl told her quietly.

"D-dead?" Ivana exclaimed.

"He killed himself with poison when he was discovered. We caught him entirely due to you," the Earl went on. "He had arranged to have the Prince Regent killed at his party last night."

"How could you have – known from what I – told you that it was – what he intended?" Ivana gasped.

"You told me the two things that really mattered," the Earl replied, "that Pier would enter

~186~

the house by the garden door, which is on The Mall and that the Marquis told him that His Royal Highness would be dressed in the uniform of a Field Marshal."

"Just two – words!" Ivana murmured.

"Two words that saved us from what would have been disastrous for the morale of the Duke of Wellington's Army and indeed the whole country."

"So you were – able to – save the Prince Regent?"

"*We* saved him," the Earl replied, "and now we are not going to think about it anymore but enjoy the fruits of our victory."

"I-I can hardly – believe it," Ivana sighed deeply. "It is – so wonderful after being so – frightened that Lord Hanford had – found me and that I can now be – with you."

She looked a little anxious.

"Y-you did – really want to – marry me? Not just because you were – saving me from that horrible – wicked man?"

"I married you because I love you as I have never loved anyone in my life before," the Earl answered, "but I will tell you more about it when we arrive at our secret hiding place."

To Ivana the whole drive was enchanted from the moment they set off.

They had only a little over twenty miles to go and they stopped at midday and ate a small luncheon at a charming country inn,

It was a simple meal, but it had seemed to Ivana like the Ambrosia of the Gods and the home-brewed cider was sheer undiluted nectar.

It was after four o'clock when they entered a drive of lime trees.

Ivana saw at the end of it the most beautiful house that she had ever imagined and she was to learn later that it dated from Tudor times.

It was black and white on the outside, while inside there were low ceilings made of oak beams and diamond-paned windows.

It looked out over the loveliest garden that she had ever seen.

"This was my grandmother's house," the Earl explained as they drew nearer to it. "She was a keen gardener and made the garden into one of the loveliest in the whole County."

"It is so enchanting! Everything is – beautiful!" Ivana enthused.

"That is what I felt when I saw you," the Earl murmured quietly.

Because of the expression in his eyes, Ivana blushed and he then added,

"Do you realise that we have been married for a very long time and I have not kissed you yet *as* my wife?"

"I-I want you to – kiss me," Ivana whispered.

They entered the house and the old building smelt of roses and honeysuckle and also of lavender and beeswax.

The rooms were filled with furniture which, Ivana was to learn, had been collected by the Earl's grandmother over many years.

One or two of the servants called the Earl 'Master Sebastian' and they were obviously delighted to see him.

The Earl took Ivana upstairs to the room that had been his grandmother's.

It was the prettiest room she could imagine and it was filled with vases of flowers.

When she had fallen asleep the night before, the Earl had sent a groom to tell Nanny that Ivana was safe with him.

He had sent another groom to warn the staff at his grandmother's house to expect them.

As Ivana looked round the bedroom, she saw endless lilies-of-the-valley, Madonna lilies and white roses.

She recognised that the Earl had chosen flowers that were symbolic of their Wedding.

"You have – thought of – everything!" she sighed.

"I thought of you," he answered, "and now, my darling wife, because we have driven so far, you must rest before dinner. I do know that Mrs. Maynard, the cook, will have been preparing something special for us since the early hours of the morning."

Ivana laughed.

"It is obvious that all the servants here love you."

"They have spoiled me ever since the day I was born," the Earl said, "as now they will spoil you."

He looked at her for a moment before he went on,

"Get into bed, then I will come and tell you what I wanted to tell you last night but you already had gone to sleep."

"That – was very – foolish of me. I-I so wanted to stay – awake so that – you would kiss me."

"I will make up for it now," the Earl promised.

He left the room and an old housemaid came bustling in to help Ivana take off her wreath and her gown.

"It be ever so excitin', my Lady!" she said. "And we're all thrilled that his Lordship's come here for his honeymoon."

"It is the prettiest house I have ever seen," Ivana enthused. "I hope we shall come here very very often."

"That's what we 'opes," the housemaid grinned.

She produced a pretty somewhat diaphanous nightgown that might have been sent with her by Mrs. Meadows or perhaps it had belonged to the Earl's grandmother.

Ivana did not wish to ask any questions, all she wanted was to be alone with the Earl.

He came into the room and she looked at him in surprise.

He was wearing a long red robe frogged with black braid.

"Are – you going to – rest too?" she asked.

"I hoped that you would allow me to do so," the Earl answered with a faint smile.

Ivana blushed.

"I-I thought perhaps – you had come to – talk to me," she suggested.

"I have something far more important to do than talk," the Earl replied.

He took off his robe as he spoke and then climbed into the bed beside her.

"I want to kiss you," he said, "and, my darling, my precious little wife, I want a great deal more, but I am afraid of frightening you."

"How could I – ever again be – afraid of you?" Ivana asked. "I prayed and – prayed for you to – save me and, like an – Archangel sent – from Heaven, you came to rescue me!"

The Earl pulled her closer to him.

"That is what I want to be to you and, my precious one, we are the luckiest people in the world to have found each other. In fact I thought that you existed only in my imagination. But now we are never going to run away again to love because we two have already found the sublime love that we have both been looking for."

"And I – only wanted to be – married if – I loved someone – as Papa and Mama – loved each other," Ivana said. "When I overheard Step-Papa – selling me I knew that I – could not live and – be with a – man like Lord Hanford!"

"Of course not," the Earl replied. "At the same time, my lovely one, you have to forget him. The only man you have to think about now is me!"

Ivana laughed.

"How could I – think of anyone – else?"

"I will not allow you to do so!"

Then he was kissing her, kissing her possessively and demandingly until she felt as if he took her very heart from her body and made it his.

Then, as the bees buzzed outside the casement windows and the birds sang like angels in the trees, the Earl very gently and lovingly made Ivana his.

As they discovered the ecstasy and rapture of real Love, they were both transformed.

They were no longer on earth but in the sky amongst the stars.

They had found the Love that only comes from God and is part of God.

And it was theirs in their hearts and souls for all Eternity.

OTHER BOOKS IN THIS SERIES

The Barbara Cartland Eternal Collection is the unique opportunity to collect all five hundred of the timeless beautiful romantic novels written by the world's most celebrated and enduring romantic author.

Named the Eternal Collection because Barbara's inspiring stories of pure love, just the same as love itself, the books will be published on the internet at the rate of four titles per month until all five hundred are available.

The Eternal Collection, classic pure romance available worldwide for all time.

Printed in Great Britain
by Amazon

15953329R00120